Red Creek

Book 1 of the Maro Prakk Novella Series

By: Kyle Belote

Copyright

Red Creek: A Maro Prakk Novella
Copyright © 2024 Kyle Belote

Edited by: Jonathan Oliver
https://reedsy.com/#/freelancers/jon-o

Book Cover by: Ivan Zanchetta
https://www.bookcoversart.com

Author:
https://www.outpostdire.com/blogs
http://patreon.com/OutpostDire
Instagram: Outpost_Dire
Twitter: @outpostdire

Dedication

I dedicate this book to the members of House Eti. For those of you who got a glimpse of Maro in his original story, I'm happy you were eager to see his beginnings.

Acknowledgements

Many thanks to the members of House Eti who read the various drafts of this work. I know it's hard reading the same thing numerous times, but you helped me craft a better story. To my alpha and beta readers, who absolutely detested the first draft, thanks for not giving up. And to my editor, Jon. It's hard sticking with the grimdark worlds I create, but you trudge on like a trooper.

Epigraph

Sometimes darkness mars the soul for an eternity, and no matter what good deeds are done afterward, nor how much repentance is sought, it'll never wash all the stains away.

Chapter 1: One Fine Fellow

Blessed are those who serve the people, who protect the weak, who guard truth, who lay down their lives for the fellowship of all. In my eyes, they are the genuine servants in life, and may they ever be the masters in death—the Book of Compassion, The Sacral Compendium.

The sharp stench of a fresh pile of shit hit Maro's nostrils. He stopped fiddling with the saddle's girth strap and glanced at the ground behind his horse. There, a soft mound lay undisturbed.

Maro shook his head and grunted. "Ain't you a bastard?" He nudged the steed, moving him away from the defecation, and readjusted the stallion. Now, his horse stood parallel with the road instead of perpendicular. Luckily, the gentle breeze blew the scent away from him.

A rancorous laugh drew Maro's attention, and he lifted his head up from his fiddling. Three drunken soldiers stood half a dozen paces away on the saloon's walkway. The faded and peeling white paint behind them and the rough weathered boards of the sidewalk stood as testament to the shambles of Tepress. The soldiers caroused with whiskey bottles in hand, their uniforms stained from labor and drink. Maro could almost smell the spirits on their breath from here.

Glad I gave up drinking. They're fools.

Revulsion shot through him at their behavior; their cheer turned his stomach.

What latest atrocity are they celebrating? The fire from a week ago?

A few buildings had been set ablaze, charring the people inside, but that didn't matter to the army, not when they got their quarry. With the wind just right, he could still catch a scent of the burned remains. Barbarity was permitted, if it brought profit or good public relations. While serving, he'd seen leaders order them to steal cattle. Meat fed them, and they sold the rest.

I've seen a lot of shit, too much for a lifetime.

One soldier kept his musket slung on his shoulder, retaining positive control of the weapon.

I'll take small miracles when they come.

He had to. Big miracles never manifested. Not divine intervention, nor the grace to make it to the privy on time in the dead of night. That all boiled down to luck.

The other two soldiers had long given up discipline and leaned their muskets against the side of the saloon where they procured the booze.

With a shake of his head, Maro went back to tightening the girth strap around the belly of his coal-black stallion. It wasn't his business, not anymore. He used to be one of them, a soldier, a man with a mission, justified by a cause, empowered by an officer's fervor. Had they been his men, he'd have them digging latrines until their backs broke. But now, as of this morning, he was a free man, a drifter and vagabond, a rudderless vessel in a sea of uncertainty.

He snorted to himself. *A man? No, I'm a boy no longer wet behind the ears, and not a good one at that!*

But he'd killed too many people to be a boy anymore. The army quashed all his innocence. Perhaps now, just a world-weary youth riding on the cusp between adolescence and adulthood. He knew that for a lie. The years hadn't been kind, but he'd lived them all the same. No, he was a man, but his stupidity for believing in people and lack of awareness when they duped him for their vile purposes, made him juvenile.

His eyes lifted upward in silent apology to the Everlasting Autarch, if one existed. That'd been a mistake, glancing up. Despite the overcast sky, the light wreaked havoc on his eyes, but sensitivity always plagued those with the boon of fire. Eyes closed, he lowered his head until his eyes stopped burning.

Damn it.

He'd have to buy a wide brim hat before he set out for the day. The army took his when he resigned.

At least they let me keep my skivvies.

Maro peered down the street. Above the rooftops of houses and stores, all shingled in earthy tones of browns, tans, and grays. He could see the sharp peak of one of the religious temples jutting skyward. Though too far to make out which, from the cursory glimpse of the dark color and harsh angles, The House of Retribution and Morality came to mind. Then again, he never paid attention to any holy house not his own.

If I went in, the gods would strike me down. There's retribution for you.

He averted his gaze, ashamed, and a touch of heat inflamed his cheeks. Some dark things marred the soul for an eternity, no matter what great deeds a man does afterward, or how much he repents—it'd never wash the stains away. Walking into the Houses of the Gods didn't sit well with his encumbered spirit, and he'd probably never do so again.

He hadn't given up on religion, just the hope of redemption.

Those thoughts weren't productive now. Other worries occupied his immediate fate. His knotted stomach tightened as he pondered his ambiguous future.

Where will I go? What will I do now that I handed in my musket and medals for the coat of citizenry?

"Excuse me, my fine fellow," a voice said from behind him, small and timid. Maro blinked a few times as the words tumbled in his head. "Sir?"

Maro felt a gentle tug on the back of his thin, tan coat. More surprised than annoyed, Maro faced the stranger. He was shorter than Maro by a head, but the tall hat sitting over his pate almost made them equal. Where Maro stood like a scarecrow, thin and gangly in proportion, this man's stocky build espoused a round belly of hearty eating. His soft, line-less face came as a stark contrast to Maro's haggard visage, prematurely aged for his ripe twenty-three years.

Maro's dark eyes drifted over the stranger, noting the quality of his blue shirt, gray waistcoat, and matching trousers. His black leather shoes shined with the luster of recent conditioning, and the fresh manure the man stood in would make his servant embittered by further care.

The man smiled through his thick, graying mustache, and he removed his spectacles with a flourish, jabbing toward Maro as he spoke. "My fine fellow, my name is Avardi. If you don't mind, I spoke to Lieutenant Townsend earlier, and he mentioned you. I've got to admit, you look quite the capable sort. Would you be interested in some work?"

"You're standing in shit," Maro grumbled. His low and grating voice came as a side effect from years spent screaming at fresh recruits joining their battalion. He spun back to his saddle as the man exclaimed and jumped out of the droppings.

"Eh," said the man with disgust. It took him a moment to recover himself, and Maro imagined him trying to fling the excrement from the sole of his shoes. The ex-soldier patted his belt line, feeling for the hunting knife he always carried, but didn't find it. He dug through the saddle bag nearest him, searching as the man spoke.

"As I was saying, I spoke with your old lieutenant, and he's right, you seem to be the capable sort. I'd be much obliged to hire you." Coming up empty-handed, Maro glanced back at the man.

"What sort of work? You know I ain't in the army anymore, right?"

Touching his mount—which Maro called Bastard—on the rump to not spook him, Maro circled behind the beast to the other side and the hanging saddlebag. He opened the top and began perusing.

"Yes, and it's all fine. A simple job. Pays twenty-five crowns. I need you to escort young Maribel to her next of kin."

Maro frowned and glanced up. "Maribel?"

A young, tiny girl, no more than six, stepped out from behind her rich counterpart. She had dark brown hair—almost black—that hung straight and fine, with large, vibrant blue eyes. Maro gazed at the girl. She wasn't like him, sporting the warm olive skin tones of the Cosam ethnicity, nor the ashen hues of the Rennim, the pasty Miums, nor the darker complected Sional. In fact, he couldn't tell where she hailed from. His scrutiny made her clutch the doll in her left arm with a stranglehold.

The mixed heritage Ocabu?

He noted her golden brown tones, like caramelized sugar.

"No."

"But, sir—"

Maro shook his head and plunged back into the pack. "Not only no, but hell no. Not even the Everlasting Autarch could force me."

The rich man made a holy gesture in the air, no doubt indigenous to his House. "Sir, you blaspheme!"

Maro found the cold handle of his blade and tugged, working it from the saddle bag. Once out, he pulled the knife free of the sheath, and he inspected the steel. Again, without thinking, Maro gazed skyward and regretted it a second time that day. He lowered his gaze, clamping his eyes shut as the stinging subsided.

"He hasn't struck me down yet," Maro said, referring to the master-god. His eyes tracked over to Maribel. "I never professed to be a holy man, and I don't babysit snot-riddled toddlers. Besides," he gestured to his face, "is this something that poor child needs to see every day? It'll give her nightmares."

Avardi's lips moved, he peeked back at the young girl, and then took a step toward Maro. "I think she'll take a few nightmares to get to her kin alive. And she's not a toddler! She's ten!"

Maro inspected Maribel again. "Scrawny thing." His scrutiny shifted to the rich man. "Do you know anything about children?"

Avardi shook his head.

"She'd be better off with the people of her House." Maro sighed, returning the steel to its sheath. "Where's the girl's parents?"

Avardi lowered his voice. "Dead. Caught in the fire five days ago."

Maro grunted, knowing what Avardi meant. While Maro hadn't been involved in that incident, it was one more barbarity he couldn't stomach, and the catalyst for why he resigned. Somehow, somewhere, someone got a wild hair up their ass about the town sheltering rebels, a loose assembly of country bumpkins standing up to the town magistrate—utter nonsense, of course, but that's what they'd been reduced to since the Frontier War officially ended.

His eyes drifted to Maribel, an orphan thanks to the orders of officers appointed over him. Maro turned his attention back to Avardi. "Where's her kin?"

"Over in Red Creek."

"Gods' wrath! Red Creek? Are you mad? You want me to go cross-country and through the wilderness with a little tyke—"

"Sir, there's no need to be inflammatory or use such language in front of the child!"

Maro ground his teeth, then shook his head. "No, sorry. You've got the wrong man. I don't do children. Perhaps if she were older, knew how to cook and watch over a campsite …" Maro shook his head. "The trail ain't no place for a girl."

"There's no place for her here anymore."

Maro eyed the man, his gaze darting over him, resting on the bulge of the man's gut, then said what bubbled up inside him. "You could take her in by the looks of it. At least that scrawny thing would eat well."

Avardi bristled, his face flushing a shade of red, but saying nothing, he spun on his heel, grabbed Maribel by the arm, and stormed off. He more or less dragged her like an unruly dog by the leash. Maro noted the man stepped in the shit again, but he just didn't have the heart to tell him.

"What's all that about?" someone called behind Maro.

He turned and regarded the soldiers watching the tail end of the exchange. Maro didn't bother to reply. Grabbing Bastard's reins, he ambled down the road in the opposite direction.

Chapter 2: Charming Lad

Anger in my name must only be with just cause; petty anger for the sake of personal gratification is a rebuke of all that I value—the Book of Balance, The Sacral Compendium.

Maro traversed the wide dirt street; Bastard trailed his right shoulder but didn't fight the gentle tension of the reins. You could tell a lot regarding a town by the roads they kept, and this one had little more than packed dirt covered in putrid puddles and small mountains of manure. No one bothered to clean the streets, which foretold the miniscule hope for Tepress.

At least Bastard made his own contribution.

Bastard was the only possession Maro kept from his time serving. The horse, too old for battles, would soon become a burden to the roving soldiers. Since Maro resigned without warning, he forfeited any further pay, but they let him keep the stallion slated for slaughter. In the end, he came out better. Bastard still had a few years of travel left in him, and once Maro figured out his life, retiring the poor fellow to the field only seemed sensible.

I can do at least one kindness. That'll be decent of me, right?

Besides, Bastard was the skittish sort, like his rider.

The nakedness of walking around without a musket and sword wore Maro down, but it'd be a feeling he'd have to acclimatize to. His eyes darted over the pedestrians going about their lives. Women wore pluming skirts and bonnets over their hair, perhaps a shawl around their shoulders or necks. The men wore trousers and shirts, or some type of overalls. Boots were a way of life here. Maro shook his head in wonderment at their simple lives without worry. None hurried as they milled about.

How could they be indifferent about life?

It was hard not to see them as mindless, bleating sheep in need of shepherding, but the military drilled that reality into his head on the front lines. Outside the idyllic lifestyle bubble of denizens, wars erupted, food stores were plundered, possessions tactically acquired, and murderers always kept their doors open for business for a quick coin.

Maybe I should become a lawman?

It seemed a logical choice, especially when the thought settled so well with him. He didn't have any qualms upholding the law. In his estimation, lawmen were integral for protection and prosperity. Nothing thrived in lawlessness except the strong. The world of Atar needed people like him: a robust constitution, an unbridled sense of morality, a stiffened spine, and a stomach to get the job done. The notion settled over him like a warm coat, but the images of all the unblinking gazes of dead soldiers, the remains of guerrilla fighters, and the war-torn landscapes stole that comfort.

No, someone like me with a questionable past can't be a lawman.

That would be like asking him to preside over a trial for a murder he'd committed. He couldn't, in honorable conscience, sentence anyone for his misdeeds, no more than take responsibility for following the laws of the military: his superior's orders.

Damned if you do, damned if you don't. He grunted. *Well, that's one profession scratched off the trivial list.*

A sudden powerful gust kicked up the top layer of dirt from the ground, creating a haze in the air. Maro shut his mouth.

Don't need sand making matters worse.

He eyed a shop on the left with a sign: General Store. It was a shabby building, not quite dilapidated, but it might give way in the next massive seasonal storm. He couldn't open a goods store and deal with people all day. Mucking out stalls wasn't a viable option, a job more suitable for young lads who'd yet to sprout whiskers on their chin. He didn't know shit about being a smith. In short, his skill set limited him to taking orders to seize, detain, and kill.

Too bad there wasn't a job like that; I'd be perfect.

The throngs of people thinned now as he passed from the densely packed part of town and into the outskirts. The uncluttered buildings spread out more compared to the cramped confines within the town's heart. He never understood why so many businesses wanted to be in the center. It just meant more assholes in your way, living on top of each other, scurrying about in reckless haste. Maro knew when the time came to settle down, it'd be him, a cabin in the middle of the woods, peaceful quiet for leagues around, and not a damn wayward soul in sight. That'd suit him fine.

Maro's eyes darted over the window signs advertising what lay inside, which he found useless since the signs above the doors told him what to expect. He had provisions to last until the next town. A slight chill crept through him, and he shivered for a moment. Despite the day's warmth, cold plagued him, even in the warmer months of the year.

He grimaced and pulled his thin, tan coat tighter.

Just another damn intolerable side effect of the boon of fire.

But he didn't have the boon in full capacity, only aspects. Those with full mastery called flame from nothing. Maro could manipulate fire once kindled, and the ability to call heat was his, which became useful while sitting in a gods' forsaken shit hole while it pissed icy rain from above. The front lines weren't a frolic in the fields.

There were four boons granted by the gods: fire, water, wind, and life. Each held advantages, but the side effects of all made the wielders leery, or downright curse their existence. The range of ability varied from person to person, and Maro wasn't potent by any stretch of the imagination. If shackled with the fortitude of impressive feats, he might've been blamed for the fire that engulfed the buildings five days ago. Willing flame into existence lay far beyond his abilities, but once a spark flared, it became his.

Makes campfires easier while on the trail.

Other bonuses came with the boon, of course, and more often than not, they came in handy during his soldiering days. He saw far better than most in darkness, and sickness or poisons burned through his body fast, helping him recover where others languished for days or died. He manipulated light to a degree, making shadows darker, obscuring his presence as he had in countless situations while fleeing pursuers.

But that's where the positive ended and the detrimental side effects began. Coldness harried him every day of the year, regardless of the warmth outside, or the flames of a fire close by. Sunlight hurt his eyes, even on overcast days such as this, and despite his affinity, the daylight always made him feel weak and drained. Nights were far more preferable. The connection with flames burned inside him, and no matter how much he ate, he never came away satisfied for long, nor did he put on weight, which exacerbated his coldness. The last physical detriment came with brittle bones, and Maro broke more than a few in his time fighting.

One thing he hadn't realized as he ambled through life was its effects on his disposition. He'd always been temperamental, and his demerit of intolerance didn't help either. His mother often called him her reckless child, but he never dreamed it stemmed from the boon. Explosive anger, compulsive tendencies, feeling restlessness while he waited for officers to heft themselves off their fat ass and issue orders … all elements derived from his boon.

And having a shit personality.

"Damn the Autarch, Maro," his mother used to curse, "if you always let your passions rule you, you'll be alone for the rest of your days!"

Maro grunted. *The old nag's been right so far.*

The only companionship he'd known was with a paid woman or his brothers-in-arms, and that sorry bunch of bastards left a lot to be desired. If he ever turned melancholy about how miserable his life unfolded, or if he picked apart the discrepancies of his character, one look at the woeful collection around him made his future less bleak by comparison.

But none of that helped with the misery of feeling cold year-round, or the sensitivity to light.

Others had their own quirks thanks to the boons, and an entire field of people studied personalities of those with different affinities. Maro didn't believe in lumping so many people into categories based upon their boons, but he admitted some held merit, including him.

Maro's eyes, still roving over the shops before him, settled on a sign above the door to a building on his left: Bounty Hunter's Guild of Tepress.

Bounty Hunter's Guild?

While aware they'd always existed, he'd never set foot inside one nor knew how or why they operated. But they carried supplemental supplies he needed, and in this case, a damn fine hat, and perhaps a weapon. Maro changed course and led his steed to the hitching rail outside the double doors. Animal secured, he patted his neck.

"Alright, Bastard, you behave. No fooling about, got it?"

The horse lifted his head in response, then nuzzled the side of Maro's face.

"That's a good boy."

Maro ascended the three weathered steps to the porch and entered the shop. Bells jingled overhead as the hatch opened and closed. He stopped, his eyes widening as he scanned the wares. Hanging weapons covered almost every spare inch of the wood-paneled walls. Most were muskets of different makes and artistic styles, and they even had a few of the newer, double barrel guns—two shots at a time instead of one. At the far end of the wall, shorter, one-handed muskets hung like lazy, limp twigs next to their longer, more powerful brothers. Glass cases acted like a barricade between him and the rest of the place. Knives of all imaginable kinds, as well as ammunition, lay within.

"Morning," a voice called out. Maro turned to the greeter, a man with long, black hair sweeping past his shoulders. A pencil-thin moustache hugged the space between his upper lip and nose. From this distance, it resembled a slumbering caterpillar.

Maro grunted in response.

"The name's Horace. Anything I can help ya with?" the man asked.

Maro's eyes drifted back to the weapons. "Got a lot of beauties in here." He nodded at the one-handed muskets. "What are those?"

"Pistols. They've been making them for a handful of years now. I got to tell ya, the advances with guns in the last ten years are astounding. There's even word they've got one that shoots six shots before you need to reload."

"A musket?"

Horace shook his head. "Pistol." He nodded, his eyes darting to the handguns on the wall. "Before long, those will be obsolete. That's the way it's going now, smaller weapons." He turned away from the merchandise, and he sized Maro up. "Got your membership on you?"

Maro's lips twisted in a grimace. He opened his mouth to speak when the bells above the door chimed. Both men turned to see the newcomer, a man of average height but broad shoulders and chest, rush through the door. He sported blonde hair and crazy, icy blue eyes, and while pale, he didn't resemble the Mium ethnicity.

"Peredur," Horace greeted. "What brings you in a hurry?"

The man rushed up to the counter. "Gimme two cartons of balls and the accompanying wads and powder. Now!"

Horace held up his hands to placate him. "Alright, don't be so irritable." Horace moved off to do as Peredur asked.

Maro sized up the man from the side. A long beard hung from his chin like a curtain of brown stalactites, but nary a whisker shadowed his upper lip. Two pistols decorated his hips, one on each side. A massive knife sat behind the gun on the hip closest to Maro—the left one. Maro moved away, back towards the entrance. On the wall, hung a board covered with leaflets and sketches.

Voices rose behind him. "… rumor of the Lanton gang sniffing around …"

Maro perused the sheets, realizing they were wanted posters for criminals. He read one.

Wanted: Dead or Alive. Severino 'Tart' Tatum. Wanted for the theft of military supplies along the Barren Frontier, theft of cattle in Moisy, robbery of the Bounty Hunter's Guild in Shaerhys, and murder in Karisil. Reward set at one rune—one hundred crowns—if dead. One hundred twenty-five if alive. Any apprehension will receive a ten percent discount on your next purchase of a musket or pistol. All items in possession at the time of custody or death are at hunter's liberty.

"… you can't take on the entire gang by yourself …"

Damn the Autarch, a hundred crowns? That's what I made in a month with the army.

"… pick them off one at a time …"

For a moment, untold riches filled Maro's eyes. What he could do with those sums. How long could it take to bring in a criminal? True, he might have to navigate the trail for a few days, but to bring in a hundred crowns in a week? If he ever got tired, taking a break and living like a king for a few weeks wouldn't be bad … perhaps a poor king, but a monarch none the less.

He glanced over the poster again, noting the option for dead or alive.

Alive's more money, but a damn fine payout is coin in the pocket. I've been in the wrong damn profession this whole time!

He didn't have qualms about killing folks who deserved it. There'd been many times on the battlefield when he dealt death to the enemy. As numerous instances crept up, he questioned whether such punishment was merited, which wasn't counting the innocent people slaughtered in the crossfire. In the end, Maro pondered whether he was part of a good cause, or if he'd thrown in with the villains.

"… sent a caravan of supplies and people out. Ripe pickings, if you ask me …"

Had he not enlisted, Maro wouldn't possess his current skills. Regardless, few professions called for former battlefield butchers. If he hadn't joined as they marched out to quell the uprisings in the Frontier War, he might already be dead. Signing up came at the right time; either soldier up or turn criminal, and Maro knew he didn't have the temperament for such an undertaking.

"… on the road to Red Creek …"

An image of the little girl, Maribel, flashed through Maro's mind.

He spun around. "What was that?"

Horace and Peredur glanced at him as if they'd forgotten he existed. Maybe he didn't. Peredur scowled, his hand sliding to the musket on his right hip. "Stay out of it, scarecrow. You get in my way, I'll gun you down, too. This is my bounty."

Maro had been threatened before, by people who bluffed, and by those who meant it, both of which bothered him little. Peredur meant it.

"Got something to say?" Peredur prompted.

Maro grunted and shook his head. What did he care if someone had a fire poker riding up his crotch? Then again, the sergeant in Maro wanted to slap Peredur around like a green recruit on his first outing, blundering through the undergrowth and giving their position away.

Can't do that anymore. Not part of the army, and the citizenry would turn me over to the lawman if I did. I may not be a good man, but I ain't a dumb one.

Now considering it all, being in the military held advantages, certainly its privileges—like slapping around little shits like this.

"Didn't think so." Peredur's hand moved away from his pistol, and he turned back to the counter. "Put it on my tab, Horace."

Horace narrowed his eyes. "If ya don't come back with your quarry, ya better come back with money. This is the last time!" Maro watched Peredur's spine stiffen, his shoulders squaring, but before he said anything, Horace cut him off. "Ya got issue with it, take it up with Guild Master Drallus. And ya better think before ya open your mouth and threaten me."

Peredur deflated, but he snatched the balls, wadding, and gun powder off the counter. He turned and stormed out, running into Maro's shoulder as he left. Maro watched the man leave. The bells chimed twice overhead, and once they died away, Maro turned back to Horace.

"Charming lad."

Horace shook his head. "He's frantic. That's all. He's been down on his luck, bringing in the bounties as of late." Horace frowned. "Don't think I got your membership chit earlier."

"Don't have one."

Horace's brow lifted with surprise. "Well, I can't sell ya anything—weapons, at least."

"Here for a hat."

Horace nodded, thoughtful. "Yeah, I can sell ya one. Right this way."

Ten minutes later, and twenty crowns poorer, Maro exited and settled his new hat on his head, of a quality he'd never seen before, not even in the army stocks. To his surprise, and a prominent reason as to why he bought it, it came with a leather interior to keep his head warm. If he took care of his black, wide-brimmed hat, it'd last as many years as the crowns he paid. He ambled down the steps and into the overcast day, noticing the difference.

"Damn, that's nice."

Bastard perked up at the sound of his voice. Maro untied the horse and faced him toward the street, his head pointing in the direction opposite of Maribel, Avardi, and Red Creek.

He glanced back.

Ain't my business. I never was a good man, so ain't no reason to start now.

With a shake of his head, he climbed into the saddle and nudged the mount with his heel.

"Alright, Bastard, let's get this over with."

With the town to his back, Maro left his life as a soldier behind.

Chapter 3: No God Of Mine

Cursed is the man who does nothing while evil spreads, for one day, they too will fall prey to the sinister forces that bleed the world, and they will suffer a hundredfold for the atrocities they let happen—the Book of Malice, The Sacral Compendium.

Hours later, when Maro glanced back at the small town of Tepress, he realized it settled in a shallow between rolling hills. He wouldn't classify it as a valley, as the terrain didn't rise enough, but it nestled inside the trough. It wasn't beautiful by any means. Hard limestone surrounded the countryside, uncovered by a slight kick of dirt, and cedar trees flourished like a severe case of venereal disease—they cropped up everywhere.

Where once proud rivers flowed, humble trickles now bubbled in atrophied creek beds. Wildlife turned scarce, and crop yields brought in a small fragment of their once-plentiful portions. The changing weather patterns played the town dirty. Dust storms didn't help either. Far to the south, the wooded areas grew in abundance with vegetation and wildlife, but every year, the climate seemed to chip it away, making it recede. Maro heard rumors of caves out there, but he couldn't know for certain.

Tepress will be a distant memory in another twenty years.

Maro tallied up how old he'd be.

Damn, forty-three.

A distressing thought—his age, not the town.

Glancing back at Tepress had been a mistake. The little girl came to mind: Maribel.

Ain't my business.

But the words of the temperamental bounty hunter kept rumbling in his head like distant prairie thunder, 'a gang of outlaws on the road to Red Creek.' If Maro had to speculate on what Avardi would do, he'd find some way to be rid of the girl, ditching her at the first available chance. Her safety wouldn't be his priority, just finding a sucker who'd take the pay.

Maro dismounted in a plume of dust, taking a moment to stretch his legs and give Bastard a reprieve. Guiding the horse by the reins, the ex-soldier turned away from the town and continued walking.

The place was too damn dry for his tastes. If he could stomach the dryness, Maro would build himself a shack in the middle of the desert. At least, he'd be warm. As he stumbled over small rocks, the girl kept coming back to him.

A coach would do.

Stagecoaches provided a great way for the population to move around, especially those with no skill on the open road, those without the ability to take care of themselves.

Pay someone to sandwich you in between two other sweating, disgusting people, and all six people ride in an oven to your destination, all the while praying to the gods you don't break a wheel.

Coaches were fast, affordable, but they weren't the safest. Most didn't have a second rider, someone with a long-barrel musket, to shoot at any who'd try to rob the stage. When traveling, whether alone or not, you always risked highway robbery at the very least, and, at worst, an early grave.

Maro grunted.

Ain't no damn way to go for anyone, especially a kid.

But he wouldn't be moved by possibilities, nor swayed by maybes. He wondered, had his old man been worth a damn at all, would he have come after Maro to save him? Probably not. And if Maro wasn't willing to look after Maribel, how was he better than his old man?

I ain't.

But surely there was something the army could do? Two detachments sat in Tepress, idle manpower able to sweep through the countryside, dispatching outlaws, seizing stolen goods, and making the way safer for all involved.

Why isn't the damn army taking care of this? After the fire fiasco, they could use some positive public relations.

Maro knew they'd never do it, not without any profit in it. They'd fall back on the tired tripe of 'no orders.'

Doesn't the military have a mandate to keep citizens safe?

He could've sworn that's what he promised to uphold when he donned the uniform, so why weren't the soldiers taking care of the infestation?

Yeah, they do, just not my battalion.

Which was what sat in Tepress.

Maro's unit stood apart from the regular fighting force. Over the last few years, they'd switched tactics to combat the insurgents with guerilla warfare, and Maro, always forward deployed, tracked and reconned the area before the primary force came through. His job consisted of hunting for signs of the adversary long before they ambushed.

He peered over his shoulder, the small town fading as he navigated patches of spry grass and rocky terrain. The weeds out here, though water-starved for a month, would still be strong enough to slow a galloping horse. The spots of dirt between were almost as hard as packed roads. If you fell, the ground would make a divot in you.

Maro turned away with a shake of his head and kicked a small stone with the toe of his boot. *Ain't my business.*

Putting one step in front of the other, he put more distance between him and the town, their woes, the gang, and the child. His mind drifted back over events that helped solidify his decision to leave. He didn't love the army, the fighting, but he wasn't great at anything else. The textbook definition of his life going nowhere.

When he entered the town and heard about the torched building, something inside him broke, a dam holding back the building horrors. It was one thing to kill an enemy, quite another to burn townsfolk—an unjustifiable decision. What else could he do? Stand by and let the heathens of their battalion operate with impunity?

Ain't that what I'm doing by quitting? Now that I'm out, can't do anything, regardless.

Would writing to a local politician and complaining change things? Maybe they'd launch a full investigation into the allegations. He doubted it. Like everything else dirty and shameful, they'd sweep it out the door, making sure such rumors never saw the light.

Perhaps he should've stayed, been more vocal about the atrocities? Surely not everyone approved of their conduct? Their commanding officer didn't care, Captain Hovath. Maro never met the man, but he'd seen him from a distance.

Must be nice to be so far removed from the plebs, a bird soaring high above and shitting on everything below.

What would an officer do with a sergeant who brought up uncomfortable questions? It's not like he could ignore it. No, once voiced aloud, Captain Hovath would ascertain the validity. But that'd be the last time Maro got that close to him, not when said commissioned rank commanded a sea of lieutenants and higher enlisted men to act as a buffer.

But the captain wouldn't do anything. He'd say the right words, pantomime the proper motions, and business would continue. The captain's reputation of barbarism, and the tactics his unit employed, came from his demented mind. And again, Maro stood far removed from the main body of fighters.

The former soldier adjusted the hat on his head. Nothing decent came from Tepress, except being the catalyst for Maro extricating himself from the life he'd known. It was a damn sorry day when it took burning citizens to make him see it.

Nah, my hat came from Tepress.

Maro grunted, acknowledging one other aspect.

Running into Peredur implanted a seed of an idea. Bounty hunters made abundant money, though the life would be hard.

It'd be the same shit I've been doing for years, roughing it on the trail, killing folk who needed killing. But the job suits my skills, not that I have much.

And he'd be paid an acceptable rate, too, given the freedom to hunt like the old times.

That gives me a warm fuzzy.

There'd be no uncertainty when the enemy was an actual foe to society. The men he'd chase would be criminals—vile creatures ruled by their baser instincts. He'd be doing the world of Atar a service. A touch of hope flickered in his chest. After all the awful shit he'd done, he might turn into a decent man.

Yeah, right?

The idea intrigued him, and perhaps he'd look into it once he got to … wherever the hell he ended up. That was the problem with not having a path. Atar lay before him, but not all trails were open. He had to figure shit out and quick. Prospects came slim, and money ran out fast.

I'd whore myself out, but I'd end up paying clients to sleep with me.

He thought of going home, the town he grew up in, but there wasn't anything there for him. His mom died before he joined the military; his father drank himself to death when Maro had been but a boy, and the only thing the bastard ever did for Maro was teach him how to duck when someone threw a punch.

Maro's uncle still lived, his mother's brother, but he hadn't seen him in years, and didn't know where to look for him.

Maybe I'll wander the road for a bit?

That thought wasn't intriguing in the slightest, and it didn't provide profit either. He wanted a bed with a roof overhead, or a job that paid for all the time he'd spend away from it. The bounty hunting gig sounded more appealing by the moment.

Until you get shot.

He'd been shot before, but luck, like time, would end. If he went fast, a bullet between the eyes, well, at least he wouldn't suffer. It'd be over before he realized what happened, but sadistic little shits filled Atar, like the fighters they battled, and some men were turned into a slow-roasted pig on a spit, or skinned alive until their body gave out.

What kind of world do we live in?

Part of the problem manifested in people like Captain Hovath and his tactics. Hostiles would enact an atrocious deed, Hovath would order a retaliation, something much worse, then a revenge would happen, further escalating the barbarity and tensions.

The officer, the nemesis they fought, and the criminals, spread like a pestilence upon the world, and most didn't have the means to fight off the infection.

A weight settled over his chest.

But I do.

His lips tightened in a thin line as bile filled his mouth. Without a doubt, something in the holy *Sacral Compendium* talked about men like him, and if not, then, in the sacred texts from The House of Lust and Candor, the temple Maro belonged to. There were nine Houses of the Gods, and his was but one.

"Damn it," he uttered aloud.

Bastard gave a small nicker in response. Maro glanced at the horizon, noting how low the sun hung.

Too early to camp.

If he turned back now, he wouldn't make it back to Tepress until deep in the night.

This is why I've stayed alive for so long. Good men do stupid shit, get themselves killed. Damn, what does that say about me?

He turned to his mount. "What do you say, old timer? Still got one more fight in you?"

Bastard nickered again, this time a touch louder as if he understood and confirmed.

Maribel's face floated in front of Maro's eyes for a moment. After all the horrible deeds he let happen, he could do one right.

Still won't make me a good man, even if I do bad things for a just cause.

He peered skyward.

"Alright, Autarch. If you're listening, you know I don't ask for much." Maro shifted to the side of Bastard, put his foot in the stirrup, and hauled himself into the saddle. "If you let the girl be alive by the time I find her, I'll get her home." He turned the horse around and faced Tepress. "But if something bad happened to her, or if she's dead, I'll slaughter everyone who had a hand in it, even Avardi, and I'll denounce your ass as no god of mine. Deal?"

He hadn't expected an answer, but it felt damn fine to vent.

"Alright Bastard, we've got to make up for lost time."

Kicking his flanks, Bastard shot forward like a ball from a musket barrel.

Chapter 4: One Cheap Bastard

Blessed is the man who saves his wealth, but may he be cursed if such frugality brings harm to others—the Book of Greed, The Sacral Compendium.

Darkness had blanketed the city for hours by the time Maro returned to Tepress. If he had to guess, it neared midnight. The streets were deserted, and while the sounds of a rancorous group needled the air from a nearby tavern, it only came from a handful of voices.

Probably soldiers.

Bastard was breathing hard, having galloped the last stretch of road, and the sharp tang of his lather hit Maro's nostrils. He leaned forward and patted the steed's neck.

"Damn fine horse. That's a good boy."

Bastard's ears twitched at the sound of Maro's voice, and he blew out a breath. Maro glanced around him, getting his bearings in the night. Deciding to ensure Maribel's safety, he hadn't a clue where to go. Where would he begin? How would he track down Avardi? He had no contacts in the city, no friendly face to disturb in the dead of night. He'd likely take a musket ball in the gut if he did.

"Think, damn it," he grumbled. The horse's ears twitched. "Where would you go?" he asked. The steed shuffled in place, but he shifted and now, more or less, faced the Bounty Hunter's Guild. Maro glanced at the building, and either candles or lanterns burned within. Someone was up.

Have to be, if a hunter returned late at night.

"Damn good horse." With affection, he patted his neck again. "You're a damn fine friend."

Maro nudged Bastard toward the business and dismounted when he drew next to the hitching post. With the stallion tied, he hurried up the steps, his boots echoing off the wood in a hurried clack, clack, clack.

Whomever he found within would be leery of giving him any information. There were tactics he could use, interrogation methods he picked up in the army, but he'd do so without all the pain and violence. When dealing with unknowns, or in this case, a complete stranger, it was always best to relate to the individual. Since Maro didn't give a shit about the person inside, he'd use a different approach, finding a topic both could discuss and find common ground with. Once established, he could guide the conversation to what he really wanted to discuss.

There was a slight chance the direct route would work, so he planned to come right out and ask. If it didn't, he'd utilize the roundabout method.

His hand gripped the cold brass knob and, to his surprise, found it unlocked. A short twist later, the door swung open, and the bells chimed overhead.

A few moments after he closed the hatch, a sleepy Horace entered with a pistol in his fist. At first, his bushy brows frowned in confusion, then a scowl crawled over his visage.

"If you're here to rob the place, you'll only end up dead for your trouble."

Maro shook his head, held up his hands to show his unarmed state, and padded to the counter.

Damn the Autarch. If I rode all this way to be shot for my troubles, the Almighty's got a twisted sense of humor.

"Not here to rob. I need information."

"Try the town hall tomorrow. They open an hour before breakfast. The guild's for members only."

"How do I join?"

Horace eyed him with suspicion. "What makes ya think ya can be a hunter?"

Are you fucking kidding me?

But the question was valid. Horace didn't know him from the next poor sod who stumbled in here.

"I've got five years in the army with the basilisk dragoons. We've been fighting the uprising on the Eastern Front of Redinar wild lands."

Horace's brows quirked up. "Ya survived that hell for five years? Ever been shot?"

Gods, if you only knew.

Maro nodded. "Three times, and one particularly unpleasant. Got broken bones, too."

Horace nodded, setting the musket-pistol on the countertop. "You've got the constitution, but there's more to bounty hunting than shooting people."

Well, that's a damn shame.

Maro bobbed his head side to side. "Not to be an ass like Peredur, but I ain't got time for a run down. If I got to join for information, I will."

Horace's brows prickled upward, and his face flashed between indignation and admiration. He settled on somewhere in between. "There's a fee for joining: two hundred and fifty crowns."

Maro's eyes widened. "I ain't got that kind of money on me!"

Horace looked him over. "No doubt."

Ouch.

Horace sighed. "Alright, we can take half of your bounties until the fee's paid, then ya can be a full-fledged member with all the accompanying discounts."

"Fine."

"Got a weapon?"

Maro tapped the massive knife on his left hip.

Horace gave a single chuckle. "You're gonna die, son."

Maro shrugged. He might. If he did, at least he'd be dying doing one thing right. It didn't give him any warm, fuzzy feeling most spoke about when doing something equitable. Perhaps it was a lie people circulated to feel special. He'd given coin away to those in need, and he only felt the pains when he needed to make purchases later. He'd shared food with those who had less, and all he got for his trouble was a grumbling stomach, and much sooner than expected.

Horace scratched his chin. "Alright, we'll take your information for the processing and get ya a membership chit. Now, what do ya need?"

"Avardi, who is he, and where is he?"

Worry and caution and a touch of something else coated Horace's features. "What ya want with the banker?"

"Hmm."

Figures a well-dressed and overweight fellow worked at the bank. The damn gilded class has it all.

The common name of the rich was the gilded class, which sat at the top of the five-tiered structure of society. The merchants followed, more commonly known as the hawkers. The general population came next, touted as plebeian. The two lower rungs comprised the servant class, what the rich called the rabble, and the slaves, serfs. Slavery clung to life at the far extremes of civilization, well away from the major cities, where the gilded could pretend it didn't exist, to protect their sensibilities, of course.

"He brought a girl to me earlier in the day," Maro explained. "Wanted me to escort her to Red Creek."

"Red Creek? The Curse take that man! I told Avardi that's out beyond the wilderness and along the frontier." Horace groaned. "He tried to get the guild involved, but he didn't want to pay the hundred and fifty crowns."

"Hundred and fifty?" Maro exclaimed. "The bastard only offered me twenty-five!"

Horace chuckled. "Smart man for not taking it."

"I was tempted. Where is he?"

Suspicion entered Horace's eyes again, and something warred within the man. "What are ya going to do to him?"

Maro shook his head. "Nothing. Just ask questions."

"Why?"

"To find out what happened to the girl. If she's here, I'll take her."

"Not as a member, ya won't, not unless he pays the full price."

"Fine, I can freelance."

"And if she's gone?"

"Find out how he sent her. Peredur spoke of a gang earlier. Didn't think much of it. What's that about?"

Horace nodded, thoughtful. "The Lanton gang. Vicious bastards, the whole lot. They always seem to know when possies are after them, or when bounty hunters start sniffin' around."

Maro grunted in response.

"The terms rape, pillage, and plunder do disservice to their antics. They burn crops of farmers who don't pay, steal livestock, kidnap little girls for reasons the gods only know. Rumor is the ones they don't keep, they sell to traders in the wilderness. Course, they're really slavers. Some gals are released, scarred for life in more ways than one."

"How many of these bastards?"

Horace cocked his head from side to side. "Hard to say. Anywhere from eight to fifteen. They keep the group small, more spoils for their members. I know they kill their own if they're too weak, or they let hopeful recruits fight to the death to join."

"No lawman in these parts?"

"What's one man and a deputy going to do against a whole cabal? Besides, he ain't even here right now. Rode out to Grand Gorge for a trial."

"What's Grand Gorge? A big divot in the ground?"

Horace chuckled. "No, it's the biggest city for at least four hundred leagues."

"The army doesn't do anything about the Lantons?"

Horace shook his head. "The only thing they do is deplete our stores, but they pay ... so far."

"Hmm. For now. I take it the guild won't do anything?"

Horace sighed. "I'd love to, so would Drallus, the guild master, but we can't be doing pro bono work. Once we do, the folk around here will expect it for the next little problem that disturbs them. And the next, and the next."

"Do a town collection."

Horace nodded, then gave a shrug. "We tried. Raised a nice tidy sum of a thousand crowns. Problem was, none of the hunters wanted to take on the job."

"Cowards?"

This got a single chuckle from the guild worker. "More like smart. They were outclassed and outgunned. Even with ten of them going after the bunch, some wouldn't make it back, and as long as some members of the Lantons survived, they'd recruit and come for retribution."

Maro couldn't deny the valid points, but that was the problem with engaging the enemy. You had to wipe them all off the map, down to the last man. Like pulling weeds from a garden, you excised them from the root, otherwise you'd have to do it again in a few more months.

"The banker?" the ex-soldier prompted. Dwelling on the gang wouldn't help him now, not with valuable time wasting away.

"Ya ain't gonna kill him?"

Maro shook his head.

Horace sighed. "Alright. He lives above the bank with his wife. The whole damn second floor. Stairs are on the west side of the building."

"Thanks."

"We've got to make your bounty hunter chit, so I'll need your full name."

"Maro Prakk."

Horace grabbed a piece of parchment and dipped his quill into the ink well. "What's the spelling?"

He spelled it out and gave his information to start the membership process, but his chit wouldn't be ready for a week. He could worry about it later, if he survived. He hadn't fooled himself. He knew he might not make it back.

At least one decent thing ...

For now, Maribel needed him, and time was of the essence.

Maro turned for the door.

"Nothing foolish, right? No funny business?"

Maro paused. "Depends on how you mean."

"Nothing that'd come back on us?"

"Not unless you're talking about the gang, and that's only if I need to." Maro glanced at him. "If you're referring to the banker, nah, I won't do anything in your name. Just a concerned citizen."

Maro didn't wait for a response. He hurried through the door, untethered his horse, and walked down the main thoroughfare. At night, it'd be quieter to walk, and he didn't want suspicious folk peeking through their windows and wondering why a man rode like the Cursed were chasing him.

His heart sank when he remembered the Cursed.

Gods' wrath! I didn't even think of them, too fixated on the gang. And monsters lurk in the wilderness, too.

But he couldn't dwell on basilisks, hags, or any other dire creatures lurking in the deep. He had to stay focused on Maribel and the Lantons, if they were both going to be a problem. Once he spirited her away, and the bandits fell far behind—whether they crossed paths or not—then he could worry about monsters and the Cursed.

Damn, it's colder than I remember.

Bastard's breath plumed before him, and after a moment of pause, Maro could see his own. Not as pronounced as his steed's, but he hadn't been running, either.

If I weighed more than a bundle of sticks, old Bastard here would be too tuckered out.

The ex-soldier kept his eyes roaming over the buildings until he spotted the pale blue construction with a black and white sign that read Bank. He could've seen it without the sign, being the nicest building by far, unless you counted the Houses of the Gods.

I guess in a town this small you don't have competition or the need to name the damn place.

He tethered Bastard to the post at the bottom of the stairs and patted the stallion on the neck. "I'll be a moment. You behave while I'm gone. No horsing around."

Bastard blew a breath out of his nose and mouth, his lips quivering.

"Yeah, bad joke, but lucky for you, I don't got many." Maro glanced about, checking for people who might be walking in their direction or watching. "If you see anyone coming this way, heehaw like a jackass."

If the horse could snort, he did so now, his ears twisting backward.

Maro went up the stairs as quietly as he could—no easy feat with boots on wood. No need to alert anyone to his presence yet.

Fast is smooth, and smooth is slow.

He reached the top, took off his hat, and put an ear to the door. The wood was cold against his flesh, and his head, now free from the confines of fabric and leather, felt chilly and naked. Sounds came from within, gentle voices through the wooden door. He replaced the hat on his head, noting the soaked lining on the inside and the iciness, then knocked three times with the meaty portion of his fist.

"Who's there?" Avardi called.

He sounds damn scared. He should be.

"The man you asked to escort the girl. Open up."

"No, no, thank you. She's gone."

"Who took her?"

A pregnant pause. "Please, go away. Come see me in the morning."

Maro blew out a deep breath and muttered to himself. "I ain't got time for this shit." He glanced down at the road, making sure he wasn't overseen, leaned back, and kicked the door in. He stormed through almost at a run. From his time in the army, he learned that running in and screaming disoriented the victims. In this case, shouts would alert everyone, so speed would suffice.

The banker stood halfway between the door and the small, round kitchen table. Grabbing the overweight man by the face with one hand, squishing his cheeks, making his lips bunch up, he drove him backward until Avardi hit the table. He toppled over, his back slamming on the tabletop. Some white dishes clattered to the floor, the others were wedged between the wooden surface and the man's bulk.

Avardi's wife gasped, her hand going to her mouth. As everyone settled, she turned for a knife on the black stove. Maro drew his own blade at his hip, and when she faced him, she dropped her steel as her eyes fell on his massive hunting knife.

"Smart woman," he said. Maro's gaze swept the area to search for anyone else. He noted the piss-yellow walls, the frilly lace covering the windows, and the stained cabinets with more dishes. Unless someone sat on a privy pot in the only other room, they were alone. Still pointing the blade at her, he turned his attention to Avardi. "The girl!"

Avardi's bunched lips moved a few times, then he struggled to speak. "She's gone, I tell you. I sent her out this morning."

"With who?"

"The caravan."

"What caravan?"

"The monthly caravan from Mills Depot. They supply the forts once a month along the frontier."

"How big is it?"

"Twelve wagons."

Maro grunted. That'd be a fat prize, too tempting for the outlaws to pass up, and Maribel would be another token taken on the raid. Maro's guts twisted.

"They ever been robbed before?"

Avardi frowned, and he only answered when Maro tightened his grip on his face. "Yes, gods yes, it happens every once in a while, but they're insured and well paid."

"Is the girl insured?" he asked. Now that he thought about it, the question didn't make sense, but he was too focused on tripping up the banker.

"What?"

He lowered his knife to the man's face, the edge resting against his bulbous nose. "The girl. What would happen to her if they were robbed?"

"I don't know," Avardi squeaked from his bunched lips. He was sweating now, by the buckets from the looks of it, and his oily face became slick in Maro's grasp.

Maro leaned in close. "She'd end up dead or kidnapped, you bloody fool!" Disgust roiled through him. He had to think, but when emotions ran screaming out the door, logic followed by taking the plunge out the second-floor window.

"Any soldiers in the caravan?"

"No, a few men with muskets. Usually that's enough of a deterrent. We didn't want to make a show of too much force; that implies you have something special to protect and invites robbery."

He eased off the banker, holding the knife down by his side. "When did they leave?"

"About an hour after I spoke with you."

Maro did the calculations in his head. He traveled about four hours away before turning back. Eight hours minimum. He might be able to find them in the morning, if he rode Bastard all night, but it'd be slow going with unsure footing. If the caravan set out at first light, it'd be midday before he caught them. He ran on little sleep, and Bastard was getting up there in years. They couldn't go on forever.

"She'll be fine," Avardi assured. "They've got at least six muskets on the caravan."

"And the Lanton gang's got eight to fifteen members. Did you think about that?"

"They're back?" Avardi asked, his voice quivering with fear. "I thought they were closer to Grand Gorge."

Maro let out a deep breath through the nose. By the gods, he wanted to smack the man upside the head, beat him within an inch of his dying gasps for his stupidity, but he had to practice civility. Couldn't be too decorous dangling from the end of a rope or holed up in a jail cell until he rotted.

It'd serve me right though, not for beating the banker, but for following orders that were wrong.

"The next time you've got to send someone away, you pay the full fee instead of pawning her off on the caravan, or some drifter like me for twenty-five crowns."

What are you talking about?" the wife asked, speaking for the first time. "Avardi, is this true?"

Maro eyed her, but she fixed on her husband. "Rest easy, Bathilda," Avardi said. "The men were compensated for taking her."

"How much?"

Avardi's lips worked as he deliberated. Maro grabbed his face again, and the banker squeaked. "Sixty crowns, alright? Five for each man."

Maro ground his teeth. "There's twelve people on the caravan and six muskets? You're even stupider than I thought." He released the banker with a shove and turned for the door.

"What are you going to do?" Avardi called after him.

"Hopefully, escort a little girl home. Otherwise, I'll have to save her." When he got to the broken door, he turned back. "If I find out she's dead, I'll come back and gut you in front of your wife for being one cheap bastard. Pray she's still safe."

"You're a horrible man!" the wife shouted.

"Hmm. Never claimed otherwise."

One more assurance I can never be a decent fellow.

He hurried down the stairs, the night noticeably cooler than when he went in.

Or maybe it's my imagination.

When he reached the bottom, Bastard gave him reproachful eyes, or Maro's own guilty conscience burned bright.

"Don't give me that look," he said as he untied the mount. "He had it coming."

The horse blew out a breath.

"He can replace the door. Wasn't much of one, anyway."

Maro climbed in the saddle, and the stallion whinnied.

"Well, I didn't hurt his wife. That's got to work in my favor."

Bastard shook his head as Maro adjusted himself.

"And I didn't slap him around. Not even a little."

The steed bobbed his head, and Maro wheeled to face the road leading to Red Creek.

"The worst thing's that he might need a clean set of britches. I don't have time for your nagging. We've got to ride hard. You ready?"

The horse swished his tail a few times.

"That's a good boy."

Maro dug his heels into Bastard's flanks, and they took off down the road.

Chapter 5: Law Of The Land

Let not your enemies suffer unjustly, slight not a friend with unkindness, break not a man's heart undeservedly, torch not a woman's comfort of security—the Book of Morality, The Sacral Compendium.

The early morning light came as it always did, a stabbing pain in his eyes. Too bad it didn't bring warmth, but it revealed a pillar of smoke in the distance. The black curling plume climbed like a lazy tornado among the sparse, wispy clouds. Maro couldn't tell how far it was or how big, but he fought the urge to jump to the worst conclusion.

I ain't never had the best of luck, so why would it start now?

He wanted to hope, to be charitable with his optimism, but the pessimist in him knew what lay ahead: the remains of the caravan, charred wagons, and corpses. In short order, he'd know whether a little girl interred among them.

Of course, he prayed for Maribel's safety. He wasn't much for talking to the gods and groveling for small favors. They never answered him anyway. He supposed that wasn't true, considering all the times he begged for deliverance in skirmishes over the years. Someone had listened, hadn't they? Was it enough to turn a heathen into a devout believer?

Not Maro. He'd need divine intervention to feel the overwhelming presence of the holy ones, manifested into the physical and undeniable in the flesh. He supposed they could slap him in the face. That'd be proof, wouldn't it? Perhaps a small miracle, to be sure?

He wished to be wrong about what lay ahead, but wishes were like prayers: wasted hot breath. What had happened when the gang descended upon them? Did they come in shooting, or try to ambush them in their sleep? The more he thought about it, coming in with pellets flying sounded like a lot better way to die.

I'll take a shot to the face than the slow cut of steel on my throat.

That's how Jeb died, his companion of three years in the army. They'd suffered through the worst of atrocities together, and when they stood side by side, they could weather anything. Then, one night, as Maro slept and Jeb remained on watch, the insurgents slipped through their lines and slit Jeb's throat. It was Jeb's responsibility to stay awake. Maro had awoken to the sound of his gurgling, choking on his own blood … hell of a way to wake up.

So, Maro did the only sensible thing: he shot the son of a bitch in the face from ten feet away. The splatter from out the back of the man's head blinded his friends behind him. Maro went on a rampage with his knife and also picked up the steel that took his friend's life. Soaked in blood and gore and unidentifiable bits, he swore he'd never cleanse the stains away.

He shook those dark thoughts away. No, hope had to win out, at least for the moment. Maybe a cookfire? Or did they burn a big pile of brush to keep warm? But the ex-soldier doubted it. He'd seen an immoderate sickness in the world; his hands had been bloodied by the work, too.

"Come on, Bastard," he urged, and kicked the horse's flanks, but the poor beast was exhausted. He didn't get much life out of him, and Maro couldn't blame him. They'd ridden hard yesterday, and it'd been a full day since either got sleep or had a decent meal. Luck wasn't with either horse or rider, and the rising smoke was further than both could've guessed. Noon came before they pulled up to the remains.

Maro nearly fell out of his saddle with exhaustion, and Bastard breathed in heavy, labored pants, his sides heaving.

"Poor boy." Maro pulled the stirrup closest to him up and hooked it on the saddle's horn, loosened the girth strap all the way, and removed the saddle. It dropped to the ground. "Easy lad, easy," he said, stroking the beast.

Maro let his eyes roam over the camp, searching for signs of the girl. If the entire situation broke bad, he hoped she was already dead, so she wouldn't suffer, something quick, or an accident. It wouldn't be the first time a stray musket ball struck the wrong person.

It's not like they are the most accurate weapons in the world.

He glanced behind him, to the south, on the other side of the road. A sparse forest rose up with a multitude of cedar trees, but it wasn't dense, and no one could hide inside without being spotted. He scrutinized it, then discarded it as a hiding place. Turning back to the camp, he surveyed the wreckage.

The charred remains of a wagon still smoked with each gust of wind, but it was embers now. Only half a spoke survived the fire, which helped Maro identify the remains. If anyone said a tornado ran through the campsite, tossing the luggage around, he would've believed them, except for the missing wagons.

The attack had been clean and quick, but judging from the site, he knew if they found her alive, she'd been taken. As far as he could tell, no one survived, and it didn't look like the Lantons took the time to be too sadistic. No evidence of torture.

Maybe they wanted to be in and out before anyone else came along? Autarch, if you're listening, please don't let me find that girl's body.

He felt almost guilty for asking, then just as terrible for wishing her alive. Unless she escaped on her own and was clear of all trouble or pursuit, praying for such an outcome put her in more peril than if she were dead.

Maro grunted at the thought and stepped away from Bastard. He waded through the smoking and charred debris, the strewn chests. Judging by the remaining embers, the fires started long ago, well before dawn. Not everything burned. One wagon had been tipped on the side, and a few crates lay discarded, but as to why the outlaws had abandoned them, he could only guess.

As he moved deeper through the damage, a cough made him freeze in place.

Did that come from the left or the right?

It was the kind of cough used to clear your throat, but weak and pathetic. He'd heard it before, the type to remove liquid from your lungs, so you kept breathing. Pooling blood was troubling someone, but how long before it wouldn't trouble them anymore?

Maro's hand dipped to the hilt of his blade, and in a slow, smooth, noiseless motion, he slipped it free. Watching where he set his feet, he continued on, his eyes scanning for the person in need and for ambushes.

Gods, what I wouldn't give for a musket.

He rounded the wagon on its side and caught sight of a man slumped against the underside. Blood covered his features, streaked his face, soaked his shirt right where he held his guts close to his body. Still, despite all, he recognized Peredur, the bounty hunter itching for a fight in Tepress.

"Gods' wrath," he cursed under his breath. He fought the urge to run up to him, to help, but that's how you ended up dead. During the war, the insurgents laid traps that way, pooled gunpowder under a person or body, and when you moved them or rushed through a trip wire, it'd set off a spark. Nothing remained of those eager to help the wounded.

With slow, methodical movements, Maro made it to Peredur's side, and the bounty hunter's eyes flitted to him before resting in a steady gaze.

"Y-you," he said with weak breath.

"Yeah." Maro squatted next to him. As he did, he noticed one of Peredur's pistols lying beside him, and the ex-soldier snatched it up, inspecting it to ensure it was loaded. It was.

"Help me."

"The girl; where is she?"

"Girl?"

Maro wanted to be kind, to offer comfort in Peredur's dying moments, but that wasn't his way, and his demerit of intolerance wouldn't let him. He wouldn't lie to the man, nor would he bide time while Peredur called for his mother. In some sick, twisted humor, when perishing men went to the Autarch, a woman's name was always on their lips. Sometimes, they left a lovely maiden behind; most of the time, they sought the woman who gave them life.

The ex-soldier leaned in close, bringing his face level with the dying man. "Don't jerk my dick. There was a girl in the caravan. What happened to her? Did she die? Did they take her?"

"No—" he coughed, "no girl." He winced as some of his intestines slid out of his grasp. "Help."

Maro sighed, looking over the bounty hunter, then around him, searching for any sign of tampering. "You crawl here yourself?"

"Y-yes."

Had Peredur been mistaken? Did he not see the girl? But that didn't mean she wasn't here. Or had Avardi duped him back in Tepress and lied about putting Maribel on the wagons? Perhaps he thought if he got Maro away from him, chasing a coach with a phantom girl, that he'd give up, if he ever caught them.

Avardi didn't appreciate the lengths Maro would go to, or the urge to seek vengeance on those who wronged him.

Maro kept his head on a swivel, taking in the wreckage, ensuring no one snuck up on him. "I can help you," Maro said, turning back, "but don't fuck with me. I only care about the girl. Did you see her?"

Peredur nodded. Anger shot through Maro, and he wanted to punch the man in the face or grab a fistful of guts and twist.

"You son of a bitch," he shouted. "You're wasting my time, her time, and you're dying. Did they apprehend her or kill her?"

"T-ta-take." Peredur coughed, causing the bloody insides to jiggle in his hands.

"Who took her?"

"Lanton."

Maro groaned in frustration, knowing what future awaited Maribel. The kindest fate would be a quick death, worse if she was sold off to a slaver, and even worse still … he didn't want to think about that, not with so many sick bastards in the world, but he'd make sure there'd be fewer when he finished.

A righteous anger rose within him, white hot and blinding. He'd kill them all, every last one of them. He wouldn't quibble over the means; he'd just hurt them in ways they never imagined. His time in the army, fighting on the front lines, standing guard as they interrogated all those who survived each battle … he wouldn't need to get inventive.

"Was she alive?"

"Yes."

32

Maro wracked his brain. What should he ask? What would help him the most? "How many in the Lanton gang?"

"Eleven."

Eleven? Why the odd number? Or perhaps not so odd; one leader, ten lackeys.

"Help me," Peredur asked with a thready voice.

"Alright," Maro said, standing. He glanced around, making sure he was still alone. "I'll help you." Without sympathy or pause, he cocked the musket-pistol, aimed between the bounty hunter's eyes, and pulled the trigger.

The shot rang out, and a wisp of smoke exited the barrel. Bastard cried out from where he stood, frightened by the sudden noise, but as a horse trained for battle and musket fire, he wouldn't bolt for the hills.

Normally.

When they took him by surprise, that was another matter. He might be skittish for a few moments, but he wouldn't run off … far.

Better not.

Maro removed his hat and held it to his chest. "Sorry, Peredur, but nothing could be done."

And it was true. Maro had seen men with wounds like Peredur, and they never survived long, and if they did, they screamed in agony. Even with trained healers, few as there were, most expired. What he'd done was a kindness. Someone watching from afar wouldn't think so, equating it to nothing short of murder, but damn the man who'd never stood in Maro's boots and cast judgement. He gave Peredur a quick release, as he would if Bastard broke his leg out on the trail.

No point in suffering.

Maro turned the pistol in his hands, inspecting the weapon. He'd never seen one, other than the guild shop in Tepress. Muskets were inaccurate at best, and a shorter barrel wouldn't do the shooter any favors.

Alright, Autarch, you're testing me mightily, but I ain't fucking around. Keep that kid alive, or else. Oh, and uh, look after the son of a bitch I just sent your way, even though he's a dick.

Knowing if anyone was close enough to hear the shot, they'd come full speed, probably with guns smoking, and Maro couldn't be caught with his pants at his ankles. He patted down Peredur, searching pockets and the belt. He pulled out a coin pouch that jingled, a small, thin circular disc with BHG stamped on one side and Tepress right under it. On the other side, Peredur's name was etched.

"Bounty hunter chit?" he mused aloud. Reaching the man's waist, he unbuckled the gun belt, tugged it free, and stood.

Oh, and uh, Autarch? Since I found a gun, which I assume is your will, prepare yourself, 'cause I'm about to send a lot more souls your way.

He donned the gun belt, fidgeting until it sat comfortably on his hip. With prudence guiding him, he reloaded the musket-pistol.

Maro glanced at Peredur's boots, and they were far nicer than his own, what with the holes and thinning sole. He put his foot against the dead man's boot, finding them a match. He sighed and squatted. "Law of the Land, Peredur," he said, and began unlacing them. "Sorry about that."

Shod with new skins, Maro stood and searched for the blood trail. Peredur said he crawled this way, leaving his possessions behind. If the gang were in a hurry, they might've overlooked his gear, and that'd be a nice boon for him.

One question nagged Maro: was Peredur part of the caravan, or did he trail them? If he had to guess, he joined the group as a way to ensure he ran across them. That, too, troubled him. If he recalled correctly, and he might not, being half-starved and sleep deprived, Peredur mentioned taking them out one or two at a time.

Does the poor sod have more guns?

He traced the blood path back to another wagon, this one with a wheel broken, the axle ground into the dirt. A deep divot scored across the rolling plain. Most of the contents had shifted or crashed to the soft ground. Otherwise, it didn't seem disturbed.

Why would they? It's a broken wagon, and speed's of the essence.

Maro surveyed the site. Five wagons remained, and despite the state he found them in, they formed a half haphazard circle.

Five out of twelve. They carried off seven wagons. Guess I better find the others, see if they have anything to identify them with, but first …

He sifted through the debris, finding the dead bounty hunter's gear. The bag still had its straps, and Maro rummaged through. There were a few changes of clothes, skivvies, a few shirts, some socks, and canned fruit, smoked and dried meat, and some hard cheese.

Well, that'll plug up the strongest of stomachs.

And more, it'd keep him from starving.

He thought about Bastard, and what he'd feed the poor beast. Maro hadn't tied him up, so the horse went grazing. But they'd need water. Still squatting, he waddled forward and searched for a canteen. He found two and stuffed them in the bag.

Maro also discovered a small bottle of spirits. He gazed at the container, seeing the liquid slosh within. His mouth watered from want, and if it had a voice, he could hear it calling to him. 'Just a little sip; that's a good lad.

Everything will work out alright. You don't have to feel all those terrible things you had a hand in.'

He twisted the top off, swirling the small glass flask before taking a whiff. A spicy odor hit his nostrils, and for a moment, he remembered all the merriment that accompanied the drink. He licked his lips. A single swig wouldn't hurt, right? He glanced about him. No one was here to fall prey to his inebriated savagery.

But that sweet violence caused him to stop. He'd brutalized too many while chugging away, sucking down the vile demon in the bottle, and friend and foe alike fell victim to his bony fists, or the prickling heat of his boon. In his cups, he turned hateful, and he chose to share his displeasure with anyone close by, making everyone as miserable as him.

That's the problem with most bastards today. They're fucking inconsolable, and they want to drag everyone down to their level.

And with that thought, reminding himself he was once like those little, whiny cock suckers running rampant, screaming about how unfair and unjust the world was, he twisted the lid back in place, and stuffed it into his bag.

I'm fucking dumb, but I ain't so stupid. If I get shot, I'll need to clean the wound.

And during this ludicrous quest, he ran a damn good chance of just that.

His stomach growled, and he pulled a long strip of meat from the bag and chewed as he went on to his next stop. Three bodies greeted him, but he found a few more scraps of food and another canteen. Upon frisking the cold corpses, he came across another pistol and more coin, but the muskets were gone.

Figures they'd stop for firepower, but they didn't consider the pistols worthy of collecting? Their mistake.

He moved to the next, and on it went, adding to his stores, always frisking, keeping count. When he finished, he tallied up the bodies: eleven, not twelve.

It's not like the damn thing drove itself, so where'd he run off to?

It was possible he escaped, but Maro doubted it. Another option was that he was captured and taken by the Lantons. While that, too, seemed improbable, it was more likely than the first scenario, and he couldn't discount the possibility of the man going willingly. He mulled over the thought. Would the Lantons be smart enough to embed one of their own with the caravan—that way, they'd know which to hit and which not to?

What if they had a man on the inside but for all the caravans? Why would they hit this one?

Maro turned and surveyed the field, taking in the ruts of the wagons.

Surely they wouldn't hit this one just for Maribel?

The more he thought about it, the more unlikely it seemed. A gang wouldn't risk their lives for a little girl to sell or keep. Besides, how would they know she was on the trail? No, this attack was prompted by more, so what made this convoy more special than the others? They went out once a month, and Avardi said only some were attacked.

What drew you bastards? What am I missing?

He pulled off his hat and ran fingers through his short brown hair as he thought. He'd need to go through the wreckage again, and this time, pay closer attention than counting bodies and stuffing his bag. Maro checked all five pistols he found. He ensured they were loaded and ready for use, tucked two in his holsters, and the rest into the belt.

Hat placed on his head, his eyes wove over the ground and the tracks. He'd tracked and reconned four out of the five years with the army. He noted the horse prints, both those with wagons attached and those without. Each wagon, judging from their size and their supplies, had four to six horses a piece. That he recollected, the trail to Red Creek wasn't an arduous one, rolling hills and nothing mountainous. Four to six would be plenty, depending on the load.

He roamed through the center of the devastated camp, his eyes on the ground. All tracks crisscrossed, making it hard to parse any sense of it, but then, he saw it: ruts deeper than the rest. Focusing on that, he followed the path two dozen paces out of the shambles and almost due north.

He lifted his eyes to the horizon.

In the distance, the Shrouded Mountains loomed, a two-to-three-day journey—if he rode hard—and Bastard wouldn't finish it alive. With the thieves pulling wagons with supplies, it'd take longer.

His gaze dropped to the middle ground, noting the Blighted Forest that sprouted like a thick wall between him and the mountains, and the trees butted up against the foot of the rising slopes. The forest ran east to west for days, or even a week, depending on how far along it he was and which direction he took.

Unless there's a road, there's no way they're getting through, which means they'd have to turn off somewhere.

Besides, monsters thrived in there—gigantic serpents that swallowed men whole, combative nymphs, and the ankle-biting gnomes.

Well, at least hags aren't in the area.

Other monsters lurked inside, but he wasn't an expert. Too many roamed the land to know them all, and a vast majority were region specific. Only a few were nomadic, going where they pleased. Moreover, he couldn't discount the Cursed. They cropped up anywhere. Of all the monsters of Atar, they were the most dangerous; as creatures, they were the most like the rest of civilization because they used to be them. Anyone could become one.

Even Maro.

He glanced down at his fingers, searching for any sign of the Curse spreading, but his fingers remained unblemished.

For now.

Everyone battled with it. The Curse was innate in them all, and the more one used their powers, the more it spread. There were ways to cure yourself, for a time, but it always came back. If you let it spread too much or go too long without proper attention, you became one of them.

Maro dropped his gaze to the ground, the ruts filling his eyes. Why was this trip any different? He closed his eyes, thinking back over the last twenty-four hours. Gods, he was tired. His heavy eyes drooped, and sleep threatened to overwhelm him. If he could stand a little longer like this, he'd be fine.

Nothing to it.

The banker's words floated through his mind. *"No, just a few with muskets. Usually that's enough of a deterrent. We didn't want to make a show of too much force; that implies you have something special to protect and invites robbery."*

Maro struggled to make sense of the interaction, to open his eyes. The sunlight seemed brighter, and he winced. How long had he been standing there? Had he fallen asleep? He glanced at the ruts again.

Show too much force. Why would you care, Avardi? Why does a banker concern himself with the caravan's protection?

Somewhere in his addled mind, it clicked.

Gods, you stupid son of a bitch! You stuck a girl in a convoy ladened with money. That's why the ruts are deeper. That's how you knew how many muskets they had. Stupid, stupid, stupid!

A troubling thought wormed its way through. How did the Lanton gang know? It came back to the missing man, and the more he thought about it, he grew certain of the mole within.

You're really testing me, aren't you, Autarch?

Though it'd sting, he glanced skyward, finding the sun, then closed his eyes and pulled away. He shivered as his eyes watered. Why couldn't it be warmer? He'd have a few more hours of light, and by the time he stopped for the night, he and the horse would have been going for a day and a half. They needed rest.

Maro gazed over the wreckage. Bastard needed food, and the ex-solider to find a way to carry it. One more sweep would allow him to gather anything useful for the trail, and then, they'd start up again.

One last, hard ride, Bastard.

He hoped he didn't kill the poor beast.

I'm coming, Maribel.

Chapter 6: A Visitor In The Night

Respect the creatures around you, be they wild or tamed. Tend to them as you would the land and care for them as they labor. May your bounty be plenty, and your belly filled with their essence. Even in death, may they sustain you—the Book of Balance, The Sacral Compendium.

The sun dipped low on the horizon, a blaze of beautiful, chaotic crimson. But Maro didn't care, couldn't see it, or stand straight either. As tired as he might be, Bastard was far older and shouldered the brunt of the work. He'd alternated between walking and riding, the latter becoming shorter bursts in between long treks afoot. Soreness throbbed from his feet to his hips, and his back and neck ached something fierce from the prominent droop in his spine and lolling head.

That's what two-days' worth of sleep deprivation will do to ya.

But it also made staring at the ground easier. You had to find the bright side in the deluge of life.

He gazed down at his latest dilemma, just another trickle of shit in the flood of obstacles in his way. All the wagon tracks leading away from the ambush had used the single file method during their egress. Now, they fanned out and went their separate ways. He glanced at them all, and he could've sworn there were twenty wagons.

Damn. Can't see straight.

Maro swayed on his feet. Though there was still a bit of light left, he couldn't go any further, and he was sure Bastard would rebel if asked to continue. Maro couldn't help Maribel if he wound up dead, either by stumbling into the gang with bleary-eyed delirium, or if his steed kicked him in the head for being an uncaring prick.

His eyes shifted to Bastard. Maro's fortunes would sour if the old mount died, and catching the caravan on foot would be improbable at best. He had an affinity with the horse, a bond that got them through the hell of the Barren Frontier, and the dull expression staring back at him now dared him to climb up again.

"You'd mutiny, wouldn't you?"

His horse didn't deign to respond.

Damn, that's how tired he is.

At the caravan massacre, he found a barrel with corn, and he let the horse eat his fill. Maro filled a few rough woven sacks, tied two to each length of rope, and put them over Bastard's rump. He couldn't carry more than four, not with all the extra supplies Maro plundered. Such encumbrances would slow them down and deplete his mount's energy, being used like a donkey, a fair trade considering the alternative was death.

Maro turned, glancing out, but not really seeing anything. That peculiar feeling washed over him, when his eyes glassed over and nothing he saw registered. He shook his head, clearing his vision.

Focus, damn it.

Around them, there was little cover or concealment—the first rule of sleeping out in the wild, and he knew that better than most. A strip of bushes sat to the right, and a half dozen oaks grew clumped together on the left. Before him and to the north, the ground sloped up in a rise, and behind him, sloping away, was wide open, the trail they'd traveled.

Damn.

It wasn't hard to figure out what to do, but mustering the energy was different. Though he hated to, he'd put Bastard with the trees, and he'd find some way to crawl under the brush and sleep. By separating them, if someone from the Lanton gang returned, they'd go toward Bastard, thinking him there.

Better remove all the goods from him so I can't be robbed, mount and all.

"Come here, Bastard," Maro called, motioning him forward with a hand.

If his mount could cock an eyebrow at him, he would've done so now. But the horse didn't budge, not an inch, not even a shift in his stance.

"Son of a bitch," Maro muttered, more to himself. The horse's ears twitched.

Grumbling, Maro walked over, removed the corn, loosened the girth strap, and pulled the saddle off. He tossed it as close to the bushes as he could, but sapped of strength, it landed a pace away, nowhere near his intended target. Snatching up a brush from the saddle bag, he held it in front of the horse's face.

"You be a good boy and come with me, and I'll give you a good brushing."

An unenthusiastic snort was his only response, as if he didn't believe the ex-soldier.

"Alright, fine, a half-assed brush. I'm exhausted, too, chap." He grabbed the reins. "We good?"

Bastard gave a slow, tired bob of his head.

Leading, Maro set out for the collection of oaks. Removing the saddle before had been laborious, and he couldn't imagine having to carry it the distance between the trees and shrub. The tack would be manageable, though.

Somewhere in the back of his mind, Maro registered the heat of the setting sun, and for the first time in years, Maro felt warm, mostly due to his addled mind, something akin to being drunk and lethargic. It was kind of nice, not shivering with the cold chill turning his bones brittle.

He groomed his companion once they stood under the shade.

"I know it's been a hard road," he cooed. "And you've done a mighty fine job, but tomorrow's gonna be just as torturous. We've got a little girl to rescue. Think you're up for it?"

The horse's head bobbed. Maro had no idea if the creature understood him or not, or maybe it responded to tone and not the vocabulary, but after all these years together, there had to be some sort of understanding, right?

A dog understands his master, why not a horse? But if Bastard starts talking to me, I'll know I'm truly fucked.

After tending to Bastard for five long, excruciating minutes, Maro eyed the distance between the trees and the bushes, a mere thirty paces, but it might as well have been all the way back to Tepress.

He shivered from exhaustion. Gods, why was he so tired?

Maro hoped to find a better coat than his own among the wreckage, but he couldn't lay claim to any of them. Most were either soaked in blood or too tattered to be of use, and the former was of much higher quality than his own threadbare cloth.

He blew out a breath.

Might as well get this over with.

He toted the bundle of tack he'd removed from Bastard to the bushes and dropped it, then hurried over to the saddle and corn and dragged it close. By the time he finished moving everything, his breathing had turned ragged, and blood pulsed behind his eyes.

You're a damn fool, Maro. Running after this girl, and you don't even know if she's dead or alive.

More than anything, that told Maro how exhausted he was, the self-doubt. Maro didn't doubt, he questioned. When he woke up to the tactics used by the army, what their commanding officer ordered, he still obeyed, but not without reservations. When those inquiries went from 'is this the right thing to do,' to 'how can this be justified,' it was time to leave. And he did.

But now wasn't the moment for reflection and self-recrimination. Sleep called to him, exhaustion caressed him, and both touches were more erotic than a topless woman sitting on his lap.

And it costs nothing, too!

He glanced back at Bastard who stood motionless in the trees.

Poor beast's probably already asleep.

He hadn't tied the steed up. He wouldn't run. Bastard was trained to charge into battle, not flee in fear, so if any coyotes came sniffing around, they'd get their skulls kicked in and trampled underfoot. The problem: scavenging predators roved in packs, but Bastard would make a ruckus so large, even Maro couldn't sleep through it.

By now, the sky had darkened, the stretch of space above the horizon turning a steely gray. With a sigh, Maro shoved his possessions through the tangle of stumps between ground and leaf, then crawled in after them. He might have to rough it, but with the use of a little ingenuity. Using a bag of corn for a pillow and making sure at least two of the pistols were within reach, he wrapped his thin, meager coat around him and drifted off.

When he awoke, he froze in place, his skin prickling with anticipation. Darkness greeted his eyes, and while that hampered most, the boon of fire was his since birth, allowing him to see in darkness as well as most folks in the day. Something lurked beyond the bushes, sniffing, growling.

Fuck.

Though groggy and tired, he remembered the pistols sitting beside his head. He'd shoot whatever came inside, but at night, the sound would carry for a long way and alert the Lanton gang—if they lingered nearby—that they had a close neighbor. If any grew suspicious, and Maro guessed they would, they'd come to investigate. But he couldn't do nothing. He was at risk, and so was Bastard.

He wondered why whatever animal lurked beyond his sight came to him before Bastard. Maro glanced down, eyeing his possessions. Maybe the open bag of meat, or him? He probably stunk more than his steed.

Maro closed his eyes, focusing on part of his boon. While fire and heat played the largest role of those who had his gift, a smaller aspect was the manipulation of light—or the lack thereof—and he shrouded himself in deeper shadows. He tugged on the darkness, swallowed up his supine form, sheathing himself in a tenebrous blanket. Then, carefully, and as quietly as possible, he reached for his flint and steel in the saddle bag.

It'd be the understatement of the century to say his affinity with the fire boon was weak, unable to call flame. If he stared down the barrel of a gun, and the only means to save his life was to blind the shooter with dazzling light, he'd be on his way to meet the Almighty Autarch.

And though he couldn't call forth flame, the sparks were his to control. He slipped open the clasp; there was an almost whisper of soft of leather, and reached in. The contents shifted inside.

Damn it.

The beast outside stopped, having heard him, and the growl came back stronger. The sniffing breaths started again, and this time more eager, as if a tasty meal lay within.

Shit.

Maro almost grew frantic in his search. He didn't care how much noise he made now. The animal knew something was in here, and the eagerness, the sniffing, searching, and burrowing deeper inside left him precious seconds. The bubble of darkness kept the creature from seeing its quarry, but it did nothing to muffle the sound or hide Maro's scent. With a final effort, Maro jerked the fire starter free and up near his chest as a massive head pushed through the darkness.

Glistening fangs like ivory knives filled Maro's vision, the dark lips peeling back to show a massive mouth. The growl returned, and Maro's eyes tracked up the long, furry snout and into the luminous eyes glowing like embers.

"Shit."

The growl tumbled out from somewhere deep in the creature's throat, its lips parting, the teeth yawning open. Hot, putrid breath washed over him, and he fought the urge to gag. The fur rippled around the neck and shoulders, and death was only moments away.

He struck the starter, flint grinding against steel, and a few stray sparks illuminated the night, but that's all he needed. Reaching for his control, he engorged the sparks. One obeyed his command without delay, the others dying a silent death. Flame shot out and engulfed the creature's head.

The beast yelped and pulled back. Maro gave chase, the fire following the monster as it pulled free of the shrubs. Holding his control over the now writhing flames, he stretched them out to form a barrier between him and the animal as he crawled out, chasing the creature. There weren't many options to ensure the beast didn't come back, only fear or death.

Clear of the tangle of trunks and limbs, Maro stood to his impressive height, and for the first time, he witnessed the monster in its entirety. It was massive, all muscle and fur, and menace oozed from it like piss from a terrified soldier. Maro's bowels turned watery, fear running through him like white water rapids.

Well, I'm fucked.

And that was enough. A dam slammed across his rushing terror, and years of training, detachment, and the will to survive clad him in armor.

I can do this, I can do this ...

The beast took the form of a massive wolf.

It ain't no wolf.

Nor was it a dire wolf, and both were bad in their own right. He stared across the flames, noting the subtle differences. Its long claws were hooked like a hawk's talons. Black fur started at the feet and turned smokey gray at the spine. At the shoulder, the monster reached Maro's stomach, but the long neck and glowing eyes gave it away.

A warg.

Once the realization set in, the terror returned, causing Maro to lose his control; the flames faltered, sputtered out and died, cloaking them in darkness. The eerie glowing eyes moved in the night, dropping lower to the ground, telegraphing the impending attack. Maro clicked the fire starter again, and he reached for the sparks, but they eluded him.

"Fuck."

He clicked once more, and the embers faded before he could grab hold. Maro's bowels quivered, and he almost ruined his britches. All went quiet; the moment when a hunter pounced on its prey.

Fucking Autarch!

Maro struck the flint and steel again. In panic, in desperation, he pushed with all his might, demanding, willing the flame into existence. It answered his call, and Maro flung the flame up, a towering wall stretching wide and high as the warg leapt. He ducked and rolled out of the way; the beast missed him, but its fur caught fire, enveloping its stomach.

Maro came to his feet, his pulse pounding, his breathing hard and sporadic. The warg thrashed in the bushes, yelping and rolling as the flames licked its underside. Maro had half a mind to kill it, to roast it alive, but he wasn't cruel nor sadistic. Reaching out for control of the fire, he called it to him. The blaze leapt from the beast and into Maro's waiting palm. A glowing ball formed in Maro's hand, and he watched the warg.

Your move buddy. Run along.

Self-preservation was an instinct so ingrained in creatures, impossible to overcome. No matter how much training men had before they went into battle, some turned and ran, others huddled in frozen horror, and some hid. Now was one of those times where survival should manifest. Pain was a lifelong and instant motivator.

The warg made its feet, jerking in the direction of Maro, its glowing eyes low to the ground, its hackles rising, the rumble in its throat returning.

"Son of a bitch."

The warg shifted, its paws facing him.

"I won't be kind this time around."

The warg's shoulders trembled.

"Really?"

It leapt, claws extended, mouth open.

Maro flung the ball of fire in an underhanded toss and leapt to the side. This time, the flames engulfed the beast. When he made his feet, he poured his will into the fire, intensifying the heat. When the warg hit the ground and rolled to a stop, only a charred, smoking husk remained. It didn't even whimper, dead before it came to rest.

"Damn it," Maro said as the stench hit his nostrils. Its fur would've made a fine pelt and kept him warm at night. And the meat could've given him strength and several meals without digging into his reserves.

A tingling shot through the fingers of his right hand, and he jerked them up to inspect them. The tips under his fingernails turned the familiar blue-black of the Curse. It was expected, but still, every time it happened, it always took him by surprise. He'd used his boon, more than what was natural, and he'd start to pay the price.

But he wasn't worried, not yet.

In the past, he'd let the Curse stretch to the middle knuckles before cleansing. No matter how much or little the Curse spread, you didn't turn your nose up at it, uncertain where the point of no-return came, where you'd become one of the Cursed. Now manifested, it'd spread quicker with each use of the boon.

He sighed, a breath escaping from his nose, and he let his hand fall to his side. Too awake to go back to sleep, he glanced at the eastern horizon, which glowed a fainter color than the sky above.

Dawn. Damn, it doesn't feel like I slept at all.

Maro turned to the oaks. The whine of a terrified horse hadn't awoken him, so either Bastard never saw the attack coming, or he slipped away like a greased pig squirming through the hands of a butcher.

Maro made it to the trees, and to his relief, he didn't find the gnawed remains of his companion among the dirt and roots, but he also didn't see Bastard.

Too dark to find him now.

While Maro's sight was enhanced at night, it wouldn't allow him to see as if through a spy glass. Maro wanted to call him with a whistle, but he still didn't know how close the Lanton gang was.

Sighing, he returned to the bushes to pull out his possessions. Bastard was well trained, and he'd come for the food. He'd return, or he wouldn't, and fretting about it wouldn't change anything. If he hadn't come back by full light, Maro would have some tough choices to make.

Chapter 7: Butcher Shop Hog

Let those who are filled with hate speak what's in their hearts, for you will heed it in their words, hear it in their voice, see the facial mars of anger and bitterness, and they'll be revealed as one without logical thought or a heart worthy of weeping over—the Book of Malice, The Sacral Compendium

Bastard returned just before full light. Wherever the hell he ran off to, Maro couldn't guess. Despite all the training and battles, the horse would stop for food. When mealtime came, he devoured all in his path, far faster than what was healthy. If a stranger watched, they'd think he hadn't fed the animal for days.

Bastard came trotting up to the cluster of oaks, staring at Maro, daring him to complain.

"Well, at least you're smart enough to return to the food."

Bastard shook his mane in response. He fed him, but giving him water turned both simple and complicated. Since Maro didn't have a pot to cook in, he turned his hat upside down and poured water inside. The leather lining held the water rather than let it seep through. He reformed the hat more like a bowl and poured in a little from a canteen. When the horse drank it all, he poured in a little more. The only damnable part? Putting the wet thing on his head afterward, but it couldn't be avoided.

Both watered and fed, Maro saddled Bastard, mounted up, and returned to the ruts. Picking up the trail of the heaviest wagon, he followed.

The rolling hills all blurred into a familiar and repetitive landscape. Sporadic shrubs popped up in unexpected places like zits on his ass. A few trees claimed their territory with an impressive display of dominance in an otherwise less-than-hospitable environment. Their towering trunks with wide, splayed branches proclaimed to nature that nothing could fuck with them. Maro kind of liked the symbology. Rocks peeked through the ground, and to the bounty hunter, it seemed like the entire terrain was covered with a thin layer of dirt, encasing the hard limestone beneath.

No wonder no one farms this wide-open land.

Unless others knew about the creatures prowling at night, and that's why they stayed away.

The warg came to mind.

With the deadly encounter behind him, and with all his years of reconning in the army, he realized his pitiful knowledge of the terrain. If he was to become a bounty hunter, and he still wasn't sold on the idea no matter how enticing the money, he had a lot to learn.

More training? Am I ever gonna be done with it?

His whole life turned out to be nothing but one long, continuous, and never-ending session of learning not to shit himself, memorizing his letters and numbers, how to dress and match colors, formal education, the army, how to shoot his musket, build a fire, care for wounds …

Damn miserable experience.

The only enjoyable part was the sweet comforts of a woman, but that'd been a long while since his last tutoring session.

Perhaps he'd need to team up with someone in the beginning stretch of his new career? The idea rankled him. He hated people in general. The young boys in his unit were different. They obeyed, and their fears kept them in line, of reprisals, disobedience, and punitive action by Captain Hovath.

Ruthless bastard, but spending years out in the wilderness, chasing ghosts and heathens will change a man.

But Maro didn't want to lose all his civility, just most of it. If others thought him a monster, it was because they didn't know him. He did have morals, otherwise he wouldn't have left the army, or be scouring the gods' ass-end of Atar to find a missing girl. Despite not caring about the frivolity of other people's lives, a little girl's safety gnawed at his conscience.

I'm coming, Maribel.

He tried to push her out of his mind other than his need to hurry and rescue her. Sparing her from a life of whatever the Lanton gang planned would pay a little of the debt he owed the world of Atar for associating with the army and all the terrible things he did. True, he fought a pernicious enemy who was deadly and barbaric, but Maro's unit answered in kind.

If in the end all you do is blind and maim each other, what life is left to enjoy afterward?

When he put it in that context, thinking of each battle as part of a body, he'd be blind, deaf, and an amputee. If confined to a bed for the rest of his life, force fed to keep him alive, he'd hope someone would have the decency to put a bullet between his eyes like he did Peredur. Thinking of the dead bounty hunter didn't bother him. It was the kind thing to do. Perhaps others wouldn't see it as civil, but he saved the man excruciating hours of misery, dying a slow death because no one would have the stomach to end the suffering.

He wondered if he'd feel the same if it was Maribel. He shook his head, trying not to fixate.

The landscape didn't change much as the hours trickled by. The rolling plains shifted to more hilly terrain, and there were more clusters of trees the closer he drew to the forest. While still a solid two days away, the vegetation suggested the things to come. Crooked, proud oaks jutted out of the ground, almost surrounded and choked off by the cedar trees. That gray mossy shit grew over the bark, and the leaves faded from a lustrous hue to a pale green.

The bubble of a creek caught his ears, and he came to a halt to judge where the sound came from. Down at his feet, Maro peered at the tracks. A wagon had stopped here for a short while, the ruts deeper in one area. Squinting his eyes, Maro noted the earth turned a rich brown and clumped together. Even the limestone underneath disappeared.

Bastard's ears twitched, hearing the moving water, too. Maro took a quick glance skyward. They'd been going for several hours by now, still tracking the same meandering ruts.

"Let's take a break, huh?"

He dismounted and laid the reins over the horse's neck. And Bastard, being Bastard, took this as freedom to amble around, following his master to the bubbling creek. As he neared the rolling brook, Maro stepped on some loose, smooth rocks, stones that used to be underwater, which caused his foot to slip.

A frightened, pained voice called out. "Fellas? Is that you?"

Maro froze, his brow cocked. His eyes scanned the banks on both sides of the creek.

"Bobby?"

Maro slipped the pistol on his left hip free and moved it to his right hand. If he was entering a shootout, he wanted the gun on his right hip available for a quick draw, instead of trying to pull from across his body. With cautious, light steps, Maro moved forward. The closer he drew to the creek, the rockier the terrain turned.

"Guys? I knew you'd come back. Help me!"

The voice came from his left, along the creek. Maro stepped over the rocky bank; the clatter of pebbles underfoot shifted with each step. The only consolation to the ingress was that the rushing water drowned out most of the noise. If lucky, Maro would be on top of him before he realized it.

Drawing closer to larger boulders hiding the person crying for help, he squatted low so his head wouldn't be seen until the last moment. By the time Maro's eyes fell upon the man, the stones were waist high. In a glance, Maro noted he stared at a dying man. The bandit, pale faced and beaded with sweat, lay on his back, the upper part of his shoulders and head propped against the rock face. The man's charcoal gray coat was draped over him like a blanket.

That coat would look mighty fine with my black hat.

"You're not Bobby," the man said.

Maro grunted. "Not Bobby."

"Who the hell are you?"

"I could ask the same, but I know who you are."

The man frowned, suspicion etching his face. "You know me, stranger?"

"Not you personally, but I recognize a turd floating in the river when I see it." With his left hand free, Maro used it to vault over the rock and land between the man's legs. With the toe of his boot, Maro lifted the edge of the coat away, revealing the tourniquet on the man's right leg, and a quarter of the way up the thigh. Maro removed the coat completely, tossing it aside so he could see the man's hands. He sat weaponless.

Not that it'd help much. With blood loss and weakness, he couldn't shoot Bastard in the hindquarters from ten feet away.

Maro's eyes scrutinized the wound. "Looks like a love bite. Want to tell me what happened?"

The man scowled. "No. A disagreement between me and a friend."

Maro grunted. "That friend be Bobby?"

The other didn't say anything.

"Or would that friend be someone guarding an ambushed caravan from a day ago?"

The man's eyes widened a fraction before he schooled his features.

"Thought so," Maro said. He lifted his eyes to the surroundings, making sure they were alone, and no one snuck up on them. He'd seen variations of this kind of ploy, someone pretending an injury, or they were injured, and their mates took the helping stranger unaware. Maro glanced over his left shoulder, back towards Bastard. In greed, the steed drank from the creek without a care in the world.

Shouldn't let him hog the sauce, but I've got other things to take care of at the moment.

The ex-soldier turned his eyes back to the dying man. "The tourniquet's the only thing keeping you alive. Looks like a nicked artery. Tell you what," Maro said, spitting on the ground and stirring it with his boot, "I'll help you in exchange for information."

A wary expression crept over the man's face. "Like what?"

Maro pulled his hat off, taking his time, his hand reaching inside and reshaping it, letting the damp leather breathe. He squatted down and stared the man in the eyes. "The Lanton gang. You are—excuse me—were part of it."

The man opened his mouth.

"Don't deny it," Maro cut him off. "I may look as ugly as a mule, but I'm not as dumb as an ass. Now, I don't care what you stole. The way I see it, if you don't protect what's yours, if you're too weak to stand your ground, maybe you don't have the constitution to live on the frontier." Maro paused. "Sorry, getting carried away with my philosophizing while you're here bleeding out. Guess that's the only way I can get anyone to listen to me." A grin tugged at the corner of Maro's lip. "A captive audience, you might say."

"Listen, mister—"

"The girl," Maro said, a grating hardness entering his voice. The other man went still. "Where is she?"

The man's mouth opened and closed a few times. "I don't know what you're talking about."

Maro drew the long hunting knife from his belt. The steel glittered in the sunlight, blinding him.

Damn sun.

"Now, I ain't a barbaric man by any stretch of the imagination, at least not in my natural element; I like peace, prosperity for all, and no one telling me what to do, but we don't live in a fantasy world. So, I've learned my lessons the hard way, and after you get hit in the face enough, you remember to put up your fucking hands and protect yourself."

Maro sighed, then with a single shake of his head, he said, "I've seen and done shit that'll make your asshole pucker. Spending five years in the army on the front lines teaches you a lot about a man, what he's willing to endure, his resolve, the cause he fights for, and what parts you can cut off to make him squeal like a butcher-shop hog."

"Grace Autarch," the other man said in a shaky breath.

Maro shook his head. "God ain't here, only me, but I understand the confusion." Maro took two hunched, waddling steps closer. "I only care about the girl, what happened to her, where they took her. So, I'll make you a deal. I'll stop cutting when you tell me what I want to know."

The man's eyes went wide.

Maro grunted. "I'm glad you see my resolve and the seriousness of the situation." Maro lowered the knife to the man's shin, to the soft muscle resting beside the bone. "Now then, the little girl. Is she alive?"

"Yes!" the other said with a sense of urgency.

Maro let out a pent-up breath.

"Is she healthy and whole?"

The other man nodded. "Last I saw."

Maro grimaced. He didn't want to clarify his question, but … he had to know. "Your gang's full of a bunch of sadistic bastards, so I'll only ask this once. Did any of you rape her?"

A look of horror crossed the man's features. "Grace Autarch! She's just a little child. Like seven."

"She's ten, no need to be inflammatory, and I noticed you didn't answer my question." Maro pushed the blade into the muscle.

The man's lips parted to scream, and with his free hand, Maro threw dirt into the man's mouth. Caught between screaming and choking, the body did the rest. He coughed and hacked and spat the dirt from his mouth. Maro withdrew the blade, the tip coated in blood.

"Now then, the girl?"

Once the man got control of his body, he answered in a rush. "No, we didn't touch her. She had to be pure for the buyer."

"What buyer?"

"I don't know his name," the man answered in a whimper. "Ludre never tells us more than we need."

"Who the fuck's Ludre?"

The man's eyes widened in shock. "He's the leader. How do you not know this?"

Maro shook his head. "Should I?"

"Aren't you a bounty hunter?"

Maro shrugged. "New to the profession and these parts. I don't give a shit about Ludre, just the girl. Where is she?"

"They took her to the meeting point, Double Rock Ranch."

Maro sighed. "Where in the hell's Double Rock Ranch?" Maro shifted the knife to right above the man's ruined knee, and the man rushed to tell him.

"It's to the north and west of here. Not far from the tree line of the forest, near Salt Canyon."

"Northwest? Toward the wilderness and Red Creek?"

The man nodded, his eyes bulging. "Yes, please, don't hurt me."

Maro frowned. Torture was never a sure thing. Half the time, the prisoner spouted shit to make you stop cutting, and to be fair, he'd barely done anything to this man yet. For all he knew, this outlaw spun yarns to nowhere. "And what about the money?"

A frown flickered over the man's face, but it wasn't an immediate reaction. There'd been a delay. "What money?"

Maro grimaced. "Damn the Autarch. You *had* to lie to me." Maro reached for the man's hand, stretching it out. His prisoner tried to fight him, but Maro won the round by breaking his arm, then he deftly removed the man's pinky. He would've done just the tip of the knuckle, but the struggle irritated him.

In the end, after a handful of shallow stab wounds and losing three fingers on the left hand, the man told him everything he needed to know. Maro wiped the blade on the man's shirt.

The criminal wept, cradling his mangled hand with the other.

Part of Maro was repulsed by what he'd done. In the past, he'd only watched as interrogations happened, stood guard while the enemy screamed, cried, and spilled their secrets like blood on the front lines. Whether admitted or not, the icky feeling in his gut started the staining of his soul.

I'm damned, anyway.

If ever a chance for redemption, Maro doubted he could pay the exorbitant cost plus interest. But a slim reason for hope remained. He'd left Captain Hovath's battalion, which ran amuck and counter to the regular army. Their small units were forward of all operations, and he took command on the frontier, where the guerilla fighters and bizarre tactics ran rampant.

Maro left the sadistic butchery behind, the senseless waste of life, but perhaps the ghost of those atrocities still followed, a proverbial ball and chain, forever shackling him prisoner. Knowledge was one thing, but he took no pleasure in what he'd done. He wasn't like the interrogators in his old unit, the ones who had a bad day if there wasn't someone to cut, pummel, or drown in a sobbing mess.

Can't focus on that. Maribel's still out there.

And it was true. The girl needed his help, and Maro, before he set out on this quest, promised the Autarch he'd kill everyone involved. Shooting a man in the face was impersonal, business, but removing parts of him while he wailed was something else entirely.

"Calm down," Maro said after a time. "It could've been worse."

"Worse?" the outlaw croaked, scarcely audible with his pain-riddled voice.

Maro nodded, then squatted in front of him. "I've seen the worst of what humanity has to offer. Of course, it didn't start that way, not at first. That's what happens when you throw in with the wrong people, and they turn you into a fanatic like them. It's one word, one idea, one deed at a time. It's a slow process, but a long con."

Maro glanced around them, still ensuring they were alone. Someone might've heard the screams and came skulking.

"First time I saw an interrogation, they were punching him, softening him up. He spilled his secrets; they always do. There was sleep deprivation, starvation, dehydration, forced labor, you name it. The last one I witnessed, they turned the man into a eunuch. So, yeah, it could've been worse, like cutting your balls and shaft off and feeding them to you. Be glad I ain't them."

And Maro knew with certainty he would've done so if the scoundrel revealed anything untoward about the girl or her treatment. But the secrets the man spilled to save himself left Maro feeling hollow. Had they been worth the cost to his soul? He could wrestle with the philosophical quagmire once he rescued the little girl.

He stood, the pain in his legs reminding him that squatting for prolonged periods wasn't the best idea. What Maro learned illuminated much of what he speculated. He'd been right about a man on the inside for the job, but he'd been wrong on the count. They had a man riding with the caravan, but the one who pulled the strings was the rotund banker in Tepress.

Fucking Avardi!

He stood atop as the mastermind behind the plan, telling the gang where to go, what to hit. While this Ludre might run the outfit, he answered to Avardi, 'cause without him, they relied on sheer dumb luck. What turned Maro's stomach even more was that Avardi wanted Maribel unblemished for himself. And after his sick fun, he'd either sell her off to slavers, or kill her to keep his secret.

By the Autarch, I told the man to keep her! Maro closed his eyes and shook his head. *I almost damned the poor girl forever.*

But there was still time. She was alive, unspoiled, and would remain so until Avardi came to collect.

"You're not gonna leave me here to die, are ya?" the man whined. Now writhing in pain and panicking, his accent bubbled to the foreground.

I was never a good man, and this is one of the reasons why.

Maro glanced down at him. "Yes."

The man's face went slack with terror and disbelief. "You can't!"

Maro squatted again, put his knife to the man's mangled leg, slipped it beneath the tourniquet, and sawed it free. "Watch me."

Once the bandage split, Maro plucked it up and flung it behind him. He heard a faint splash as it landed in the water. The blood rushed through the artery, coloring his pants. It'd be a minute or two, and he'd cease breathing.

Maro stood as the man cried out, babbling nonsense, clutching the crimson flow.

I told you, Autarch. If I took this job, I'd be cleaning up the filth and sending them to you. I keep my word. If you want to smite me for what I've done, you can do it after I save Maribel. Maybe, for once in my life, I'll do something right.

But good men perished. That's how every story went. The smart ones, the evil bastards, the cowardly, they all survived while good men leapt to the front to die. He leapt to help a little girl now.

This task might end up being his last. While much remained that he wanted to do—lay with a woman from all corners of every map known in existence, lose a fortune or two—he'd be content if he went out with this one deed.

The ex-soldier held no delusions, however. He might be doing a righteous thing, but he used deplorable means to accomplish it. Did that balance out or tip the scales? He wouldn't be privy to the knowledge until he stared up at the Autarch and received his judgement.

Maro blinked, realizing the man wasn't moving. He'd died while Maro mused over the finite details of his soul and deeds.

That's probably how my end will go, as silent as the trees swaying in the wilderness, and as dignified as a wet fart in the britches.

Glancing to the left, he spied the charcoal gray coat he'd discarded earlier.

That really is a nice coat. Hope it ain't ruined.

To the man who bled out, he said, "Sorry, law of the land."

Maro peeled off his shabby, thin coat and donned the newer one. Made of thick wool, it was much warmer, but he'd find something to bitch about before long. Maro sifted through the man's pockets and possession, coming away with little. It seemed his friends picked him clean of anything noteworthy.

He stood up one last time, took off his hat, and muttered a little prayer. "Sorry, old chap. Wish things weren't the way they were, but you did your works, and I did mine. Autarch, if you're listening, judge him fairly."

Maro donned his hat, turned on his heel, and promptly puked. The bile built with each cut, and now that the moment passed, the realization of what he'd done kicked in. He supposed it was a good thing, hacking up his guts. He hadn't lied about seeing a man removed from his member, and the butcher who'd done it laughed about it afterwards. Maro wasn't as sick as him, and he never wanted to be.

When this is over, if I survive, I'll mend my ways. No more of this torture shit.

He glanced skyward, speaking to the god he'd never seen.

But that doesn't mean I still won't kill a man deserving of it.

Turning away, he headed to Bastard and the stream. He'd drink 'til bursting, refill the canteens, and hit the trail. He wasn't far behind the gang, and he could move faster than a laden wagon.

But more importantly, he knew where they were going.

Chapter 8: The Promise Of Sweets

Revel not in atrocities but find those who do; dispatch them with haste and celebrate their demise—the Book of Chaos, The Sacral Compendium.

After the death of the tourniquet man, Maro spent the rest of the day cutting a path in a northwest route. If lucky, he'd run across a surprised, gold-ladened wagon tonight. That was the intent at least, and if he learned anything as a soldier, nothing ever went to plan.

The landscape still rolled like hill country, but the troughs ran deeper the further north he traversed, doubly so for the peaks. The dirt changed from a light brown that kicked up with the faintest breeze to the heaver, richer umber tones of fine soil for harvesting. Didn't matter though, not with all the evident rock everywhere.

Maro pondered over the death of the maimed gang member as they plodded along, and he couldn't find a shred of remorse for letting him die. Torturing him was … different. Had the Autarch made him this way, or was it the environment and people he subjected himself to? Surrounded by such individuals for five years in the army played a major factor, right? With four in reconnaissance, killing unsuspecting enemies did more harm to him than he cared to admit. If he survived rescuing Maribel, what kind of existence awaited him? How would someone, with bloodied hands and death marring his soul, slip into the bustle of life?

Moments like those stretched for an eternity as he rode in silence, the sun drifting ever closer to the horizon. He hadn't said a word since departing the creek, and most people would assume—had there been any witnesses—that his deed gnawed at his gut. And it did. No, killing him didn't warrant much thought, but Maro's actions and choices did.

He swore once this task was completed, he'd mend his ways, find remorse to repent, and he'd be earnest, but what would keep him from going back afterward? If the situation grew dire, the stakes high, would he backslide and employ the same tactics again?

In the eyes of the citizenry, killing was as bad of a deed as they came, but in his gut, Maro recognized torture to be worse, especially if you let them live. What kind of life was that, one where you walked around afterward—if you could—knowing what you'd lost? Maro would eat a bullet rather than be an invalid.

In between mulling over his philosophical quandaries, his mind turned to the duty before him. An entire gang needed killing, and preferably without firing a single shot. A successful outcome all depended on how his next few encounters went. The odds stacked against him, but he now had an advantage.

Thinking back to his time in the army, being informed turned the tide of most battles. Yes, surprise worked in their favor, but the information he and his unit supplied to the main force gave them a critical edge. He didn't have any recon units, which meant he'd either go in blind, or he'd have to do his own. So, waiting for the cover of darkness was the smart move, long after they ate, and when the majority slept. Ten members remained, plus Avardi at the end. The portly fellow would be a freebie. No indolent banker would get the drop on him. But it boiled down to the word of a dying man, one tortured for details. He would've spouted anything to make the pain stop, which was why Maro had to be sure.

And that meant cutting on someone else.

His squeamishness didn't come from doing the deed, but rather knowing what kind of person it made him.

If you don't pretend to be decent, you won't be disappointed.

Only the Autarch knew how many men he'd watched suffer the same fate over the years. At this point, it was like saddling a horse; done numerous times it came without a shred of critical thought, and it quickened his pulse about as much as trying to pass his constipation in the wee hours of the night.

Not a good feeling—how unbothered I am—not the inability to shit.

The swarthy sky brought him out of his reverie, and he pulled on Bastard's reins. Twisting in the saddle, he surveyed the surrounding terrain. Up ahead, a small strip of trees stretched across ground, and by what the dead gang member told him, that was known as Herod's Gate. Maro's gaze drifted to the right, further north, and the Shrouded Mountains loomed ever closer, as did the Blighted Forest, the latter a day's ride away. His ass puckered. He'd already faced a warg, and pretty far from its normal stomping grounds, too. What did he know about wargs, gnomes, blights, or any other creature roaming the land? He was like every other peasant in the world; he knew of their existence and nothing else.

And that made him next to useless in battle. He hoped it wouldn't come to that. There were enough problems without adding monsters into the mix.

Ten problems, to be exact.

He wouldn't count the banker.

Then, you've got to get the girl home.

The trip would take a week, at best.

Maro groaned at the path before him. *And that's without being stabbed, shot, or murdered.* Guiding Bastard with the reins, he aimed them toward Herod's Gate and gave a soft nudge to the horse's flanks. Bastard started forward at a trot. Judging by the low sun he rode into, it'd be full dark by the time Maro arrived. Rolling hills with little to hide behind stood between him and his destination, and he'd have no cover or concealment.

That's the quickest way to an early grave.

Horse and rider went down the first slope, but instead of rising up the other side, Maro turned his beast to follow the rut between the hills. It'd be a serpentine path, take longer, but he wouldn't be seen.

Thirty minutes later, both pulled up short; the sound of a wagon rustled behind them.

Shit.

When he stopped earlier, the one place he didn't check was to the rear. Had they seen him? Where he stood now, the road at his back, the passing convoy would spot him, and all elements of surprise would be ruined. Maro urged Bastard to pick up speed, to make the bend in the crevice between hills, but the going turned slow without level footing, and Bastard wasn't a goat.

Twisting through the curve and putting the road out of sight, Maro hurried to dismount.

To the horse, he spoke in a low but rushed tone. "Alright, Bastard, just like we used to. Break."

Bastard's eyes found him, and he shook his head, tossing the mane.

"We don't got time for this shit. Break."

Bastard snorted.

Maro pulled on the reins, making eye contact. "Look, boy, I know it ain't ideal, but I need you to do this. Break."

Bastard's nostrils flared as if indignant.

Maro sighed. "If you do this, and we take the camp tonight, and they got some sweets among their stuff, I'll give it to you, alright? Lie down on the fucking hill, got it?"

Bastard bobbed his head.

"That's a good boy. Now, break."

On command, the mount rolled over onto his side, leaning into the bank of dirt toward the sloping hill. Normally, he would've laid on the flat ground as if asleep, but it was either lay at an angle against the dirt, or clatter to the rocks below.

Maro followed his steed, laying prone beside him on the incline and patting his neck, leaning close to whisper in his ear, "Damn fine boy. I knew you wouldn't let me down. Now, stay."

Bastard lifted his head once as if in acknowledgement, and perhaps it was. What the hell did Maro know? When it came to horses, it was too hard to tell if they indulged him like a parent placating a squalling child, or if they were as understanding as a mutt wagging its tail.

Cats … I should've gotten a cat. Those bastards don't give a shit about anybody, self-reliant, and for the most part, they want to be left alone.

But he couldn't saddle one and ride him into battle.

Wouldn't that be something?

Maybe if he tamed a wild mountain cat. They were huge and sleek. And to think of the sheer ferocity, teeth and claws flashing with each skirmish; if anyone saw them coming, they'd shit themselves in terror.

If Bastard misbehaves again, I'll threaten to replace him.

Maro let the thought slide from his mind as he leaned against the slope and kept on his belly, crawling to the crest of the hill. Loose dirt gave way underneath his chest and limbs, making the brief ten foot climb difficult. He stopped well short of the edge as the noise grew ever louder. He'd wait until they passed and hope they wouldn't have someone on horseback trailing their precious cargo. The rumble reached a crescendo, and Maro noted voices, but not what they were saying, drowned out by the rhythm of the creaking carriage.

Maro tried to decipher how many he heard, or if he detected Maribel's voice among them, but he only found disappointment. The rush of noise pushed past him, clamoring to the left and on towards Herod's Gate. Maro counted to thirty, straining his ears, listening for any distinct clattering of a solo rider.

When he didn't hear any, he let out a breath and eased up to the crest of the rise. His eyes broke over the plain, and the wagon came into view.

That's when he heard it. He froze. The clamorous galloping rushed toward him. With slow care, he twisted his head, catching sight of the rider. The wagon, now thirty paces further along the path, rolled to a stop. A solid fifty meters, maybe a touch more, separated Maro from the group. The lone rider, however, didn't break stride, passing at full speed as he rattled over the wood bridge spanning the creek bed.

On the other side, and in a plume of dust, the rider pulled up on the reins.

"Well?" the driver asked. He wore a red shirt and stood gazing down at the trailing lookout.

"Nothing. But I swear I saw someone earlier."

"Probably a trick of the light. We're driving into the sun."

"Ain't no trick of light. I saw someone."

The driver chuckled. "Well, if we stumble across him, I'm sure the four of us can take care of him."

"Five," the lone rider said, "unless you think I don't count for nothing."

"What took so long?" another asked.

"It's this damn mare. She ain't cooperating."

Another spoke. "She's in heat. What do ya think, Boss?"

The driver didn't speak and resumed his seat. "Come on, boys. Another thirty minutes to Herod's Gate, and then we can have a nice hot meal." He slapped the reins against the team of horses, and the wagon lurched forward.

Maro dipped back down, sliding down the edge of the slope. A little cloud of dust kicked up, and rocks tumbled down. Bastard gave an irritated snort as it rained down on him.

"Sorry, old boy," Maro said as he settled beside him. Maro debated on what he wanted to do. He could wait and follow. Once he arrived in the trees, he could scout ahead, but they'd given him as much information as he could've hoped for. Five against one. Maribel remained an unknown factor. He was certain they were all armed. Muskets were a bitch to load in the heat of battle, so he wouldn't discount their knives.

But rest had to be a priority. After closing the distance and curling up to sleep for a few hours, he'd attack as they slumbered. Waking up wouldn't be a problem. Chugging water before retiring ensured you had to pee in the middle of the night, the body's natural clock, much like the rooster in the morning.

Maro waited until the rumble turned into a whispered suggestion in the distance before he considered resuming.

"Alright, Bastard, attention."

The horse didn't move.

"What? You getting lazy in your old age or obstinate?"

The horse's head moved toward the sound of his voice.

"Oh, sleeping are you? Break's over. Attention."

Bastard gave a snort.

"Guess no one wants sweets, do they?"

At the word sweets, Bastard gained his feet, shook the dust from his mane, and dipped his head.

"Yeah," Maro grunted. "That's what I thought."

Chapter 9: A Cat Licking Its Ass

The desire a man finds in his loins for a woman should be the same as the compulsion for truth; may her carnal embrace satisfy his body, just as dispensing justice should satiate his soul—the Book of Lust, The Sacral Compendium.

Maro reached the trees by Herod's Gate as dusk turned to twilight, and before long, starlight would swallow them whole. He went to the left of where the wagon entered, to the south. After tethering Bastard, he removed the saddle. Then, fed and watered his mount. Normally, Maro didn't hobble Bastard. He was too well trained, but the ex-soldier wouldn't take any chances tonight. This close to the bandits, the last thing he needed was Bastard to leave on his own accord and seek the promised sweets.

Taking a canteen of water, he chugged half.

That'll pull me out of sleep.

Maro found a smooth patch of ground at the foot of a tree with two roots sticking up in a V shape. He wedged his neck in between to keep his head out of the dirt. Wrapping his new coat tight about him, he lowered his now sweaty hat over his eyes and fell asleep.

Several hours later, his bladder woke him, pleading for release. He made his feet and staggered a few paces away, unfastening his belt as he walked. Relieved, he returned to his camp. Bastard was awake, glancing at his rider.

"What? Don't give me that look." He sighed. "I said if we found any sweets, you could have them. We haven't gone there yet."

Bastard snorted. The darkness, the trees shifting in the wind, the chirp of crickets, and the dropping temperature made him shiver. The day might belong to mankind, but creatures ruled the night, predators and jackals coming out to hunt and feast. Nothing was more terrifying than waking up to some critter crawling across you, or the fangs of a warg smiling at you.

Scarier than waking up sober next to a two-crown whore.

Maro patted the horse's neck, then used Bastard's back as a prop for his arms, and he leaned against the horse, gazing in the darkness toward the five men. He doubted Maribel was with them. He hadn't spot her earlier when the wagon stopped, but that meant nothing. Perhaps she grew feisty, and they trussed her up like a calf. Maro hadn't heard her either. Maybe they gagged her as well? Just because she was supposed to be unblemished for Avardi didn't mean they'd let her cause problems the whole ride. If she did, they'd be tired of an unruly child.

"Bloody work ahead," he said, both to himself and his steed.

Bastard nodded.

"Like old times."

The horse craned his neck.

Maro glanced at him. "Could be Maudlin Ridge all over again."

Bastard's ears flickered backward.

"I didn't like it any more than you did, but orders were orders."

Maro hated falling back on that excuse. Sure, people cast stones after the fact, but when you voiced dissent in the moment, you found the barrel of a gun in your face and an ultimatum to do or die. Maro hadn't known anyone to swallow a bullet, not when they loved living.

Bastard faced the front.

"A lot of folk died that day," he mumbled into the darkness, "but not any of ours."

The bitter taste of imaginary bile rose in Maro's throat. Maudlin Ridge had been one of the biggest blunders he had a hand in. The camp was supposed to be filled with enemy combatants, and it was, but also populated with family members.

Women and children.

Maro's recon unit swept in during the wee hours of night and subdued the majority without issue. One person per abode. Maudlin Ridge got its name from the palladium miners who all went there to strike it rich. They built a small town, but less than two years after, all left poorer than when they arrived.

Once the main body of the army closed the gap, his unit pulled out and continued on. The massacre that happened in the wake of his departure was the first inkling he wasn't on the right side of the confrontation. Now, in retrospect, even with just cause, he didn't believe war had a right side. Sure, there could be a cause, but every soldier was someone's son, father, or sibling, and no amount of violence or victories changed that.

He sighed. "Maudlin Ridge, then."

Bastard snorted.

Another massacre awaits.

The difference now was that he had no reinforcements, no army to sweep in after and subdue everything. Working alone, he couldn't keep any enemies at his back, even tied up. He'd have to kill them. The men warranted death for what they'd done, taking Maribel. Hell, if even half of what Horace had said—the guy running the Bounty Hunter's Guild in Tepress—was true, they all deserved to die, and he had no qualms about that. His dilemma stemmed from the assumption that once he quit the army, he left that life behind.

You can't go off to fight and come back wholesome. No one's the same.

But when did this become his war?

When you let a little girl jerk your heartstrings.

He sighed.

Women are trouble at any age. That's why I pay them to go away after the fact.

He glanced down at his fingers on his right hand. The Curse still clung tight, and would remain so, until he visited a brothel—the only way to cure it, for adults.

Would you rescue the kid if it were a little boy?

Probably. Maro had yet to father any children himself, but after seeing all the horrors he had a hand in, perhaps he'd raise a son or daughter to be better. And if he wanted to be a father, he had to start somewhere.

And after you kill this entire gang?

Water washed away the stains of blood, but the filth clutching his soul would have to wait until the Autarch took his life. They'd square up then, but for now, he'd just have to settle for being a dangerous man.

Pondering over it, little separated him from the criminals. The only difference came from the ethics instilled in him from the army, and his childhood before that. But even then, he saw the moral corruption and the rot amongst the ranks, and he wanted no part of it. Perhaps he was a good man?

Then, why am I still alive?

Good men died; there were no two shakes about that. He wasn't clever, nor a coward, so what did that make him? Villains always seemed to survive.

Am I the bad guy?

He knew punishment awaited him, whether from a judge, the law of the land, or the Almighty Autarch himself. One way or the other, there'd be a reckoning, and there'd be a price to pay.

But what would the cost be?

He was already willing to die. Atar would have one less pestilence to worry about. He feared the comfort of life, the change to walk the righteous path, because one day, the bill would come due, and the price would be more than he could bear.

"Alright," Maro said to the stallion. "Let's move closer, but I go in alone."

It made sense to move the camp closer. The last thing he wanted to do when finished with his work was to trek all the way back to collect his things. Horse ladened with possessions, both traipsed through the woods, drawing ever closer.

When Maro saw the first orange flicker of fire between the trees, he stopped and moved Bastard out of sight. They had to be thirty meters away. Maybe further. By the time he tethered and removed the saddle again, he discovered another problem. It happened when he placed the saddle on the ground.

Bastard was aroused.

"You've got to be shitting me," he muttered to himself. Then, he remembered. One man of the group said the mare was in heat.

"Damn it."

Bastard grew antsy, turning his head, searching.

"Hey, big boy," he said, coming to the horse's head. "We ain't got time for this, alright? I thought you were too old for this shit."

Maro wondered if he'd ever be too old. He shook his head. No, he'd never reach that age. Even if the flesh couldn't rise to the occasion, the salacious itch would still crawl through his veins.

Still, the longer he delayed, the more agitated Bastard would get, then his element of surprise would be gone. What came next would be ruthless, and it had to be carried out with precision and no delay.

Alright, Autarch, if you don't want me to send these tainted souls your way, now's the time for a sign like a bolt of lightning, or some mystical creature that talks to me. Otherwise, open up your doors, 'cause this is gonna get nasty.

Checking his musket-pistols one last time, he tucked them away in his belt. He wouldn't be shooting unless he had to. Pulling his knife free of its sheath, he waded forward and descended upon the sleeping men.

The work went quick, and most only woke up as the blade entered their throats; he kept the red shirt man for last. As the leader of this outfit, he'd have all the answers. The trouble would be in breaking him, but Maro's skills would ensure cooperation.

The red shirt man woke up when Maro straddled him, but he was rendered unconscious with a right hand. Knocked out, Maro bound the man's hands in rope, then cut away his clothes, which proved harder than expected. Tied and naked, he dragged the man over to the wagon, then with another length of rope, bound him to the wheel through the spokes.

By now, Bastard's whining grew loud and restless, and the wagon leader woke from the sound. His eyes fluttered open long enough to see Maro squatting near him.

"Good," the ex-soldier said, "you're awake. You'll want to be for what happens next." He stood. "I'll give you a minute to admire your friends, then we'll talk."

He stepped out into the darkness, working his way back to Bastard. The stallion appeared agitated.

"Easy boy." The bounty hunter stepped close and patted the horse's neck. "Alright, I'll give you a choice. We can hunt for sweets, or you can rut yourself silly. Take a moment to think about it." He waited a few heartbeats, then removed the harness that kept Bastard in place. The horse bolted through the trees in search of the mare.

Maro grunted. "Yeah, I'd pick the same." He returned to the tied man.

When he saw Maro closing in, he shouted, "Do you know who I am? Do you have any idea who you're fucking with?"

Maro stopped at the man's feet. "No, I don't know who you are, and I don't care. But since it's important to you, why don't you tell me your name?"

The man's lips twisted. "I'm Bo Samine. Second in command of the Lanton gang."

Maro smiled, a rarity these days, and he made sure Bo noted it. "Then, you'll have all the answers for me. But before we get to the questions, I want to make sure you saw my handy work. I killed four of your men before I captured you."

"But—" the man glanced at one of the dead men.

"Yeah, he's supposed to be on watch; he fell asleep. That's bad for business, and he was the first to go." Maro squatted and pulled off his hat. "Now, I wouldn't call myself a sadistic man by any stretch of the imagination, but I've seen some inventive shit in my time, and I won't hesitate to introduce you to some of the more eccentric methods of information gathering. If you jerk my dick on this, you'll be sorely displeased."

Bo's lips drew into a thin line, and Maro noted the rage behind his eyes.

Maro continued. "I've already had a lovely chat with the fellow you left for dead. The man with the tourniquet. What's his name again?"

"Sebastian?"

Maro grunted. "Sebastian?" He pointed with his hat. "What kind of fucking name is that?"

"What did you do to him?"

"Nothing he didn't warrant," Maro said. "Just asked a few questions. When he lied, well, parts of his body had to depart. When I finished, he was still alive; do you know why?"

Bo shook his head.

"Because he squealed like a stuck pig. He told me everything he could, so I left him with seven fingers." He sighed, stood, and glanced out into the darkness, towards the sounds of Bastard. "The horse's getting himself on."

"What?"

Maro looked down at Bo. "My horse. He's fucking your mare. Speaking of fucked, I want you to know how well and deep you've stepped in it. See, I left—uh, Sebastian, wasn't it?—yeah, I left him alive, but I also removed his tourniquet, and I let nature do the rest." He grew quiet, rubbing the dark stubble on his jaw, trying to remember the details. "He said he disagreed with someone named Bobby. You know about that?"

"Bobby? There's no Bobby in our group. So, you did kill him?"

Maro twirled his blade in his hands. "No, nature did. Aren't you listening?" Maro squatted again. "Now, we've got a problem. Sebastian said Bobby, and you say you don't have one, and that leaves me in a bit of a quandary. So, I tell you what. Why don't I cut on you until your stories match?"

Like Sebastian before, Maro sank his knife into the soft muscle running along the shin bone. Bo screamed, and the horses grew restless at the sudden noise. He pulled the blade out, the tip coated with blood.

"Now, don't be so vocal about it," Maro said. "Besides, you might attract the wildlife."

"Fuck you!"

"No need to be rude." He stuck his blade in again, just a little higher. A thin sliver of flesh separated the two incisions. He'd work in this manner up the length of the leg, if it called for that, then come back and sever the remaining flesh if necessary.

Bo jerked and hitched. Maro knew what it felt like, the searing pain as cold steel punctured the thin layer of flesh. The blade came free, and he waited for Bo to stop screaming.

"Now then, how'd Sebastian get hurt?"

"He was shot, alright? Shot by one man on the caravan. Nothing could be done."

He mulled over what Bo said. It could be the truth. There was no way to check the validity of the statement, but there were other ways to test who told the truth.

"Since you're the number two man, who's number one?" Bo opened his mouth, but Maro cut him off. "Now, before you go spouting lies, remember, I had a chat with Sebastian before he died, gave him the same treatment you'll get if you lie to me. If your stories don't match, I'll start cutting on you faster than a cat licking its ass, and that's pretty damn fast."

He held the knife in front of Bo's eyes.

"Now that we understand each other, let's take it from the top. Who's the number one man in the gang?"

Chapter 10: Shut Up, Wesley!

Folly is a young woman's friend, or the crown of an imprudent man; both are callow and infantile. Pray they perish with alacrity, pay not for their sins, and find peace in their absence—the Book of Intolerance, The Sacral Compendium.

Maro sat motionless outside the horse pen, allowing the bushes, shrubs, and trees around the fence line to mask his presence in the dawning light. Before him, the Double Rock Ranch house stood twenty meters away like an indolent cat stretching out in a spot of sunshine. The single-story structure of rock and timber splayed out in a long rectangle. A gray and white wraparound porch with stairs leading up to the front door matched the gray stone of the abode.

Nice place. Be a shame if someone shot it up.

A wispy curl of white-gray smoke, almost invisible against the backdrop of billowy, cotton swirls, plumed from the chimney.

Might be too early for breakfast. Maybe that's the remains of the night's fire?

As if reminding him of the last proper meal and not the dried meat he consumed on the trail, his stomach gurgled at the thought of eggs and toast with honey.

Washing it down with a mighty fine cup of coffee works wonders, too.

The smoke implied cooking and not stoked to keep them warm, which would make sense in the early autumn, but that didn't mean Maro couldn't use it for warmth afterward.

Regardless of the time of year, coldness remained his constant companion, and when winter rolled around in earnest, well, he was just more miserable than usual.

He strained his ears to detect anything, any voices, the number of moving feet … Maribel. The gnawing, tearing teeth of worry wormed its way through his guts, and that's why he and Bastard rode hard to reach the ranch house. What he learned from Bo turned his stomach sour.

There were two different mindsets in the group: Ludre and Bo's leadership, and Wesley's bucking of the system. Ludre and Bo wanted to keep the profitable and often cake-eating arrangement with Avardi. In recent months, they refrained from stealing cattle, raping, and murdering, and relied on stagecoach robbery for food, supplies, and a dandy bit of money.

Wesley favored throwing off the banker's influence and terrorizing the territory from Grand Gorge out to the fringes of the Salt Canyon. Rape, pillage, and plunder was his motto, and Bo, between the screams, told Maro that Wesley wanted to 'salt Atar with blood.'

He sighed. It seemed no matter what he did, where he went, he always found people like Wesley. They were in the army, interrogating prisoners, and now they were out here on the frontier.

Wesley, from Bo's description, was younger than Maro's paltry twenty-three years, and, by Bo's reckoning, the little pompous ass wanted to buck any shackles of control.

Some men always want to bite the hand that feeds them.

But that's not what worried him. People like Wesley, they were easy to predict, follow the trail of bodies or protect the biggest assets or the weakest people in the area; the problem centered on figuring out where they'd strike next, because logic didn't roost in an outlaw's home.

Wesley, who spurned Avardi and his control, wanted to dally with Maribel. Sensing the arising dilemma, Ludre took his best three men, Maribel, and Wesley, to Double Rock Ranch, leaving Bo in charge of getting the money back to their lair. The move puzzled Maro at first, but as he thought about it after dispatching Bo and during the ride to Double Rock, he realized what it meant.

Ludre's control of the group was slipping.

Whether Wesley was popular among them remained an unknown factor, but for Ludre to take Maribel with him, and the troublemaker, meant that Ludre didn't trust any of his outfit. In Maro's reckoning, Ludre took three men he trusted most, so if Wesley made a move, they'd be there to gun him down.

No honor among thieves, huh?

Now, in a closed environment, Ludre could watch Wesley, but that meant little chance for escape if it all went tits up. Maro scrutinized the windows, noting the open white drapes.

What are the chances that only one person is awake?

Wesley?

He pushed those thoughts aside. Ludre wouldn't let Wesley take a watch this deep in the night, not with the chance of him going in for Maribel.

Unless Ludre makes the girl sleep next to him. How ironic would that be? The man who kidnapped her also fulfilling the role of protector?

After a half minute of staring, Maro saw no movement, but darkness still smothered the light. Only the softest of golden glows from a candle illuminated the house. It didn't matter. With his boon, shadows became an ally, not an impediment.

Shit, now's the best time to go in, unless I wait another day for night to fall.

He glanced to the east. The top sliver of the sun peaked above the horizon.

No, now. He couldn't wait. Who knew what would happen in another day! More reinforcements might show up, or Avardi, or worse, turn into a killing spree, so Wesley would have Maribel for himself.

Five within: Ludre, Wesley, and three others. Five pistols. He glanced skyward. *Aren't you a barrel of laughs, Autarch?*

Staying crouched, Maro hurried forward, pausing at the putrid water trough and the corner post before making the dash to the side of the house. Hunkered over, he eased up to the nearest window but didn't peer inside, just listened. A sound of metal clattering against metal, like a pan or pot on an oven top, reached his ears. This early, it might be breakfast or coffee. If the latter, it'd take a while for the water to percolate, but the aroma might draw more.

Damn, if I smell fresh coffee, my stomach's going to announce my arrival.

A muffled voice sounded from within the house. "What are you doing awake, Wesley?"

The voice that answered came back sarcastic and waspish and young. "I'm sorry, *Dad*, am I not supposed to be? Want me to go back to my room?"

"If I said yes, would you?"

Wesley chuckled. "No, cause you ain't my father." A pause. "How's the little house guest?"

"Keep your mind off the girl."

Another pause, but this one prolonged, and it lingered like the fragrant scent of the outhouse after the morning defecation ritual. The longer it built, the more pungent it grew. Though he couldn't see the men inside, the weight of the silence built like a shit storm, and he wondered who'd step in it first.

Keeping low, Maro moved away from the window and toward the steps leading up to the front door, squatting in the corner where the stairs met the porch, out of sight of anyone who came to a window or the front door. But if they rode up to the front of the house from the trails, Maro was fucked, caught out in the open. Did someone ride around the property keeping watch? He didn't think so. He'd watched the place for over an hour before getting this close.

"When's Avardi getting here?" Wesley asked, his voice holding an agitated edge.

"In a week. Mind your business."

"This is my business. You're sucking on that tit, placating that fat sow, bowing and scraping for scraps of the cut when we could take the whole thing! We should be taking what we want."

"Shut up, Wesley!"

Yeah, shut up, Wesley.

"Think about it," the young man continued. "There ain't no real law for leagues, and every time they send a posse our way, we kill them. Even the bounty hunters steer clear."

"And why do we know when the posse's coming?"

The younger man's voice dripped with disdain. "Enlighten me."

"Avardi tells us. Ain't nothing happening without that man knowing about it. He appropriates the funds from the territory to pay the lawmen who come hunting. He keeps us one step ahead of them, and in your arrogance, you'd cut ties with him."

"So, that's why you bow and scrape to him?"

"We don't bow. We keep civilized. If we acted like animals, the way we used to do things, the way you want us to run now, they'd hunt us like animals. That's why I run this outfit, and not some jackass like you."

Ludre's got a damn fine point. But aren't they already animals? Didn't they kill farmers?

Then, it fell into place for Maro. Farmers owned plots, and as a banker with his ear to the ground, Avardi would recognize future prospects for building and agriculture projects, and he'd know what land he needed to claim to strike it rich. The acres would default to the bank, the wives and children sold to slavers—the only witnesses to point fingers at those responsible for the atrocity. But that also meant they were the spoils of war, and what happened to them from the time seized to the selling came as a bonus for the gang.

Wesley, in a soft voice, said, "I don't like the way you talk to me."

A gunshot resounded, followed by a grunt and someone clattering to the floor. Maribel screamed from deeper in the house.

Grace Autarch! She's alive!

Relief swept through Maro, but so did the familiar clutch of panic and adrenaline. He pushed all thoughts of the girl out of his mind. Shouts rose inside the abode, the other three scrambling. In seconds, they'd all be standing in the foyer with guns drawn.

Thundering, hurried footsteps filled Maro's ears. "What the fuck?" someone shouted as he came into the room.

Another gunshot, and another body fell to the floor with a resounding thump.

Any chance Wesley got shot, Autarch?

But Maro knew the answer; the everlasting god wasn't the kind to respond with answers. Nothing would ever be that easy. From behind his back, Maro pulled two musket-pistols free and cocked the hammers. Best to get those hard to reach first.

Incoherent shouts rose, cutting through the morning.

That's my mating call.

Still crouched, he hurried up the stairs while trying to keep quiet, hoping the cacophony would mask his presence.

"By the Autarch, Wesley, what the hell's wrong with you? Bo ain't gonna like this."

"Fuck Bo, and fuck Avardi, too! I run this outfit now."

I ain't a good man, but I'm sure as fuck about to die acting the part …

As the remaining voices shouted in protest, Maro kicked in the front door. The three inside froze in fright and surprise. Maro's barrels zeroed in on those nearest to him. He pulled the triggers. An explosion of lead and fire rushed out towards them. Their expressions of shock turned slack as two musket balls found their mark right between their eyes.

Before the last survivor followed the falling bodies to the ground and glanced back up, Maro had dropped the empty pistols and drew the others from the holsters. The sound of them cocking drew the young man's gaze back up to him.

"You must be Wesley."

He was a young man, and to be fair, around Maro's age, but he'd guess a few years younger.

Probably hadn't even sprouted fuzz on his balls.

"You look like a Wesley, some whiny piece of shit."

Wesley had a baby smooth face, with brown eyes and hair to match. And that made Maro hate him more. His good looks and perfect teeth; a fist would fix that right quick. The lad could've been or done anything, already had the pedigree but lacked the charm. Ladies would swoon, men would vote for him in the political arena, but he turned to outlawing.

A shame the rot took his brain.

Wesley's gun wavered, paused halfway between rising and falling. He let it drop to his side.

"Smart boy."

Wesley's face twisted into a sneer. "Saul? You got the girl?"

"Yeah," a voice answered back.

Maro groaned. *Shit, six men, not five. When did the other get here?*

"Bring the little bitch to me." Then, dropping his voice, Wesley spoke. "That's what you're here for, right? The girl?"

Maro grunted. "Yeah."

"You here because you want your turn?"

Maro's lips drew into a sharp line.

"What are you? Some pissed off uncle?"

"You could say that."

Maro's gaze darted around the open room, checking for hiding threats. It doubled as a sitting area and a kitchen area. Smooth but unfinished wood stretched across the floor. The two bodies he polished off lay in a pool of blood on a royal blue rug in the center. A pearl-white sofa sat at the far side, opposite the stove and fireplace, the latter of which was lined in dark gray stone akin to the exterior.

In the hallway, a man shuffled into Maro's peripheral vision. His pistol was trained on Maro, and with his left hand, he clutched Maribel's shoulder. In her arms, instead of the doll he'd seen in Tepress, she held a puppy.

Great.

"Looks like we got ourselves a bit of a quandary," Wesley said, a grin coming to his lips. "You know what that means, right?"

Maro grunted his affirmation.

"It means a problem."

"I know what it means, jackass. I ain't as stupid as I am ugly."

Wesley gave a single, halfhearted laugh. "Ha! Humor. I like a funny guy."

The longer this drew out, the worse it would be for him. When Saul entered the room, both men would have clear shots of him with Maribel as their hostage. Things would get chancy, the outcome fluid. If he gunned down Wesley now, he'd shut the little shit up, but Saul might kill the girl. Maro's eyes flitted to Saul. He had one gun visible.

One shot.

Would he waste it on the girl, or would he shoot me?

Shifting his arms, Maro drew the right weapon away from Wesley and leveled it at Saul. "Not another step, shit sack."

Saul paused halfway down the hallway.

"He's bluffing," Wesley said. "He wouldn't shoot towards the girl."

"Want to stake your life on that?"

Wesley changed tactics. "What do you want? Money? Women?"

"Yeah." He jerked his head toward Maribel. "I want that one to leave with me alive."

"Can't have her," Wesley said. "We can give you money."

Maro shook his head. "I already got your money."

"What?" Saul said from the hallway.

"Shut up, Saul. What do you mean, you got our money?"

"Bo got real chatty last night."

Maro's arms ached. His left, pointed at Wesley, shook more than his right. Who knew holding two pistols out like this would cause him to shake? He needed to act fast.

"Yeah. Red shirt, wagon driver, second in charge. Spilled all your little secrets once I started cutting on him. Sebastian, too. Y'all let that poor fellow die a slow death. That was until I came along. Bo told me about Avardi, the farmers, their families, even the warning he gives you once the law comes your way. You give me the girl now, and I'll tell you where I buried the money."

"Shit, give him the girl!" Saul pleaded. "Ain't no eight-year-old worth this."

"Hey!" Maro snapped. "Ain't no need to be inflammatory. She's ten."

Maro's eyes drifted over the top of his left-hand barrel, focusing on Wesley, whose red face shone like a beacon. "Now, you listen to me, drifter—"

Maro pulled the trigger of the left pistol.

Chapter 11: Do I Smell Bacon?

May your hands never tire strangling the life out of evil people; pray to me if you grow weary, and I will give you strength to snuff out their existence—the Book of Malice, The Sacral Compendium

The shot rang out. Wesley went down. Maribel screamed. Shouted curses followed in the wake.

Maro dropped to a knee, spun to face Saul, raising the right musket. He squeezed off a round once the barrel cleared over the top of Maribel.

Saul fired at almost the same instant. Maro's ball sailed wide to the left. Saul's ripped into the wall beside Maro. A spray of splinters and wood fragments washed over his face. He closed his eyes against the debris and sting.

By the time he wiped it away, Saul barreled down the hall. Maro regained his feet. The outlaw lowered his head as he rushed. The bounty hunter reached for his last remaining musket-pistol as Saul drove into him, trying to tackle him. Maro used the butt of the handle to crack the back of the man's skull. He slumped to the ground, but he groaned, tried to rise. At point blank, Maro pulled the trigger and shot the man in the back of the head.

Blood splashed the wood floor.

Saul fell limp, motionless. The acrid scent of gunpowder filled the air as a wispy haze clouded the room. The screaming ring in Maro's ears grew shrill in the quiet.

Down the hall, a tiny figure peeked out of a doorway. Relief washed over him. The girl was alive.

"Maribel," he said in a quiet voice. Or at least, it sounded quiet to him. For all he knew, he shouted at her. Maybe she couldn't hear as well as him. "Come here, Maribel. Let's get you home."

He held out a hand to her, and she took a timid step into the hallway, then another, and her face went pale.

That was all the warning Maro had. Wesley seized him from behind, his arm snaked around Maro's neck, choking him. Maro's hat tumbled to the floor. Wesley growled something in his ear, but he couldn't hear. The grip around his throat tightened, cutting off his air. Wesley was shorter, so he held the leverage as he pulled Maro off balance.

Maro clawed at the arm around his neck, but a young, squirming calf couldn't be bucked. Fighting back the panic, and the certainty that he'd die, his mind—and the years of training—took over as he raced through his options.

He came up with only one. From his belt at his left hip, he pulled the long hunting knife, flipped the tip backward, and stabbed.

Wesley screamed, something shrill and girly, and his grip fell away. The knife wrenched from Maro's hand in the sudden jerk. With the constriction gone, Maro stumbled forward. He coughed, trying to suck in that sweet air. When he spun around, Wesley crawled toward the fireplace, as if in a mad scramble to escape. For a moment, confusion washed over the ex-soldier as he took in the surroundings. Wesley wasn't trying to flee. He crept for his loaded musket.

In two strides, Maro leapt on the young man's back as his hands closed around the pistol. Maro used his reach to pull it away, but to no avail. If Wesley rolled over, he'd have a clear shot. As the two wrestled, Maro searched for anything to use. Empty pistols lay around them, and absent the knife, he was out of options. He could choke Wesley as the brat did him, but that meant giving up the fight for the weapon. Maro's eyes fell on the fire poker; he thought about clubbing the little shit to death, but it lay far beyond reach.

Maro's spied the fireplace. Bashing Wesley's skull against the rocks crossed his mind, but he'd have to drag him forward, again losing the fight against the weapon. He saw his solution.

Wesley tried one more time to turn the single-shot pistol around. Maro scrambled off his back, using his legs to hold the arm down, and gripped Wesley by the hair so he couldn't pull away.

With gnarled fingers full of Wesley's brown locks, he jerked the boy's head, and the bounty hunter spoke into his ear. "I just want you to know I was never a good man."

Glancing toward the fire, he used his boon, calling forth the flame. It leapt out of the fireplace, engulfing Wesley's face and head. Under Maro's control, the flames swallowed Wesley's head; under his direction, it wouldn't spread anywhere else. He rolled away. Wesley screamed, pleaded, rolled on the floor, clawed at his face. Maro made his feet as burnt flesh twisted with mangled cries. And then, Wesley stopped moving; the screams faded, and only a small tickle of flame curled over a charred, smoking skull. White bone peeked out among the matted flesh.

Maro grunted. "I should've said bacon ... instead of telling him I wasn't a good man. 'Do I smell bacon?' That would've been better." He spat, and the saliva sizzled on the hot bone. "Tell Bo I said hi, shithead."

Turning away from the dead man, Maro found Maribel standing in the same spot, her face white with terror.

"You remember me?" he asked.

She nodded. "You said your face would give me nightmares."

He grunted. "Yeah, I did, didn't I? I bet it still does. You haven't been dreaming about it, have you?"

She shook her head.

With slow care so she couldn't tell what he was doing, he stepped between her and the burnt remains. "Did they hurt you?"

She shook her head.

"You ready to go home to your aunt and uncle?"

She nodded. "Can I keep the puppy?" She repositioned the small, squirming dog in her arms. Maro didn't remember hearing it bark, but he could've missed it while being choked, stabbing people, or when he engulfed Wesley with fire. The pup licked her face.

Maro's lips narrowed in a line. "Don't let it do that."

"Why?"

"'Cause they lick their ass, and they lick you. You want to lick a dog's ass?"

She chuckled. "You're funny, mister."

"I wasn't joking; and call me Maro."

He let his eyes fall from the girl, and he saw two of his discarded muskets. Now that he ran through the entire gang, he wouldn't need all of them. Then again, he could turn them into the Bounty Hunting Guild and maybe pocket a pretty penny for it.

"Come on, Maribel. We've got to hit the road."

"Where are we going?"

"First, we've got to get my horse, then go digging, and after that, we've got a long road ahead." He eyed the puppy and resigned himself with a silent groan. "And yes, you can bring the little pest."

Chapter 12: Red Creek

The innocence of children is a godliness that wanes with time, and as long as you live, it will never be found again—the Book of the Divine, The Sacral Compendium.

The wagon rolled to a stop outside the squat hovel, a log cabin with a thatched roof. Maro's heart sank in his gut, not at the home, but what surrounded it.

Soldiers in black coats had taken over the residence, and by Maro's estimation, a platoon's worth congregated here, thirty men, give or take.

Don't forget the asshole in charge.

He sighed, glancing around for anyone not in uniform, any who could be Maribel's aunt and uncle, but he didn't spot them. He climbed down to stretch his legs, and he swayed once he reached the solid, unmoving ground. His ass had grown quite numb over the course of the five days it took to get Maribel here.

I can't believe I brought her all the way out here for this!

The rickety door to the house squeaked open, and the asshole in charge came out in the soft, early morning light. His dazzling insignia marked him as a lieutenant, and a musket lay in his arms. Lines creased his face like cracked leather, and he looked just as hard. Of course, the frontier made folk that way, but fighting out here seemed to weather people like petrified wood. Maro hoped he wouldn't look so worn when he reached that age. Despite looking so weathered, the officer had a clean-shaven face.

The senior asshole stopped half a dozen paces away. "Help you, stranger?"

"Maybe," Maro said. "I've got terrible news for the residents of this …" he searched for an appropriate word, "… house."

He wanted to say 'squalor' or 'shit hole.' It probably wouldn't go over well.

The man nodded once. "Hate to say this, friend, but no one lives here. I'm Lieutenant Harris."

Maro frowned at the news. "What do you mean? I thought Deral and Ethel lived here." Maribel knew little about her aunt and uncle, but she'd known their names.

The lieutenant cocked his head to the side. "They might've, once upon a time; ain't been anyone here in these parts for the better part of eight months. Some of the town's folk said they died. What do you need them for?"

Maro grunted, his lips forming a grumbling line. "Shit."

The officer took a slow step forward. "I asked why you're seeking them, stranger?"

Maro sighed. "I came to deliver bad news. Ethel's sister, and her husband, died in a fire in Tepress almost two weeks ago."

"Damn," Harris said, "that's a shame. And you said you came all the way from Tepress to deliver the news? Long way."

A sinking feeling nestled in Maro's gut, what the lieutenant hinted at, Maro being a criminal, perhaps coming to rob the place.

"They had a daughter, too." Maro glanced around the property, getting the measure of the soldiers. Most were hard at work clearing debris and garbage, but some were watching the exchange. "She's alive, and I brought her to come live with them."

"Their daughter?"

Maro nodded.

"Out of the kindness of your heart?"

Maro sensed the shifting ground beneath his feet. The lieutenant didn't believe his story, but what could he say to assuage the man's suspicions?

"No, I got paid by the Bounty Hunter's Guild in Tepress. The banker Avardi cleared the funds."

"A bounty hunter, you say? Mind if I see your chit to verify?"

Shit, this asshole keeps pushing …

Maro patted his coat as if searching for it. He was about to say he must've lost it when he remembered Peredur's chit. He fished it out of his right pant's pocket and produced it.

"Peredur?" Harris asked.

"Yup."

"Where's the girl, Peredur?"

Maro jerked a thumb over his shoulder. "Sleeping in the back." He waved the officer closer. "Come on, I'll show you. Just don't wake the beast. I only got her to shut up a few hours ago."

Maro moved to the back, next to a tethered Bastard. He gave the horse a soothing pat, then rubbed his nose.

Harris glanced inside the wagon, seeing Maribel asleep against the two trunks. The little puppy she dragged with her lay curled up beside her.

"Damn," the military man said, his voice held a touch of awe. "I didn't think you were telling the truth. I've never heard of a bounty hunter escorting little girls home."

Maro grunted. "First time for everything."

"What's in the trunks?"

Maro shrugged. "The remains of her possessions, I suppose. I don't ask questions, don't get into stuff that's not mine. They told me to deliver her, so that's what I'm doing."

"Just following orders?"

The bounty hunter nodded, suppressing the groan rising within him. "Yeah."

"Good man." Harris took a few slow steps back towards the house. "As I've said, if any people were out here, they're long dead. We've been fighting out here for over a year, so outlaws might've gotten them, enemy combatants, or caught in the crossfire."

Maro grunted.

"What will you do with her?"

Maro glanced back the way he came, in the direction where Tepress lay. Then, he turned to the town still a few miles off, barely making out the buildings in the decrease in elevation.

"Well," Maro drawled out, "I reckon I'll go into the guild house and find out what they want me to do."

"I think that's smart." Harris took another step back. "Be sure to stick to the roads. It ain't safe out here."

"Will do."

Harris turned to the house and retreated inside while Maro climbed into the wagon.

Well, now what the hell am I supposed to do?

He plucked up the reins and slapped the rump of the horses with them. They lurched into motion, and Maro heard Maribel's waking grunt. A few moments later, he felt her head pop up.

"Where are we?"

"That," Maro said, glancing back at the receding house, "was your aunt and uncle's place. You remember them?"

Maribel climbed out of the back to sit beside him. "No."

"Well, according to the army officer, they don't live there no more."

"Where do they live?"

By the Autarch, how am I supposed to tell her? Hasn't she suffered enough? First losing her parents and home, getting taken on the trail...

"Oh," she said into the quietness between them.

Way to go, Maro, don't say shit and let her draw her own conclusions.

"Where are we going now?" she asked.

"Red Creek."

"What's there?"

"Not a damn thing, kid, not a damn thing."

"Then, why are we going?"

"Cause there's a Bounty Hunter's Guild; maybe they might know what to do with you."

"Avardi said if I didn't have any family, he'd send me to one of the Houses of the Gods."

Maro glanced at her. "He say that, did he? Was he nice to you?"

Maribel moved her head from side to side. "He wasn't unkind."

"Semantics."

"What's that mean? Semantics?"

Maro shrugged.

"Well, why'd you use the word?"

He grunted.

"That's silly."

"You know what game I want to play?"

"The one where I stop talking again?"

He dipped his head in a nod.

"That's a boring game. So, what are we going to do?"

Maro sighed. "Stop at the guild and see what's what."

"What?"

"Huh?"

"What's what?"

"What?"

"I don't know, you just said what's what. What does that mean?"

"Oh."

He took in a deep breath through the nose and exhaled it twice as slow. For a brief time during their trip to Red Creek, he thought about offering Maribel a chance to go out on the trail with him. This latest exchange, one of many over the last five days, proved another damn reason he wouldn't extend her the offer.

He searched for the correct words. "It means we'll see what's going on, the options, and make the best decision." Maro turned his head, checking Bastard's tether.

"Oh, so that's 'what.'"

He grunted.

Maribel grew silent, which allowed Maro time to think. She was probably right. Going to whichever House of the Gods she belonged to was her best option. She'd be clothed, fed, given education. Sure, she'd have to work for it, but there were worse fates.

Maro let his eyes roam over the two chests in the back of the wagon. When Harris had asked about them, Maro panicked. He hadn't lied to the officer—it was the remains of Maribel's, her cut, after all her pain and suffering.

By the time he and Maribel left the ranch house, he already decided what he'd do with everything he procured from the gang. Most of the horses he turned loose, but not before wrangling eight to pull the load, an overkill, but it'd be for the uncle and his wife to use as they saw fit. Now, he didn't have anyone to give the beasts to.

From the chest of money he buried, he took out three laden pouches for himself, and a fistful more for his pocket during their trek. The rest went with the girl, a parting gift for everything she endured. It'd help provide for her for years, and if frugal enough when she got older, perhaps for the rest of her life. A single coin purse would be more than Maro had ever seen, so three would let him select his profession with care. Besides, it totaled more than he made in five years with the army.

More than enough.

The weapons he divvied between the two trunks, one for him, the other for the uncle. Maro took the musket-pistols and left the rifles to him. He'd need it more out in the country, but alas, no uncle. Maro supposed he'd take the rifles back, sell them to the Bounty Hunter's Guild in Tepress. Or he could stay in Red Creek, make a life and a name for himself out in the wilderness. If feeling generous, he could let Maribel live with him.

Nope.

"You should live here," Maribel said, as if she read his thoughts.

"Ain't a chance in hell, kid."

"Why? What's wrong with Red Creek?"

"It's in the ass-end of nowhere, that's why. The only people out here are the explorers, the impoverished—"

"What's impoverished?"

"Poor. Anyway, explorers, the poor, or the ones cursed by the gods, cause if any of them were noble, they wouldn't make anyone live here."

Maribel laughed. "You're funny."

He glanced at her. "You're pretty funny, too."

"I am?"

He nodded. "Yeah, you smell pretty funny. You need a bath."

She giggled as the wagon moseyed down the path to Red Creek.

Chapter 13: The House Of Lust And Candor

Come to me with all that makes you weary, for a heavy heart can be lifted with an abundance of humility, a diminished soul restored with forgiveness, and a life granted meaning for those who truly seek it—the Book of the Divine, The Sacral Compendium.

Red Creek.

What a shit hole.

Maro could tell from a map or by the name of a place whether a settlement was worth any consideration as a viable area to live or find work.

Red Creek wasn't such a place.

Most settlements had a proper name like Tepress, a sense of something more. When destinations were named after a landmark or an attribute, well, those spots weren't worth a damn.

And so, it was true of Red Creek.

The town—if you could call it such—got its name from the red waters flowing in the oh-so-predictable creek bed, a byproduct of the iron in the hills. The buildings were cobbled together from weathered wood, and if the gods decided to fart, they'd crash in shambles. Most doors didn't seem to close. A layer of grime covered the floor in the Bounty Hunter's Guild, and when he tried to shut the front door, the glass in the windows rattled. Maro dodged mounds of manure instead of puddles of water on his way to and from the guildhall.

This place is worse than Tepress.

He hurried down the dirt road and back to his wagon. The stench of shit threatened to singe his nose hairs. The heavy scent of rain and humidity didn't help matters. He dipped his nose closer to his shirt, and the smell about knocked him off his feet.

Maribel struggled to keep up as they left the Bounty Hunter's Guild, an uncharitable place. Without a bounty hunter chit to prove he belonged, the local post wasn't willing to lift a finger. Yes, he could've shown Peredur's chit, a risk, especially if the mouthy bastard had been there. If he bluffed his way in, and they knew Peredur, well, he'd sign his own wanted poster.

A guy like that ... you'd remember him.

A wagon rolled through, being pulled by two horses, the man perched atop the seat looking haggard and backwoods. His beard hung down past his collar bone in matted clumps. Maro would bet the old codger was missing a few teeth, but whether from poor hygiene or too much inbreeding, he couldn't say. A dust cloud swaddled them in the wake of the wagon's passing.

Well, that's fucking terrific. Took her from a proper town out to this mining site. This ain't no place for a kid.

But what town ever was?

Maribel might not get an education out here, or have a fine life like she would in the larger cities, but she wouldn't be exposed to the predatory violence of men in a darkened alleyway or a seedy tavern. Sure, wildlife might be a different story, an integral part of the will to survive. Man versus nature.

"Now what?" Maribel asked as they reached their possessions.

He glanced in the back, ensuring the two trunks were there. He had to leave them. Dragging them everywhere might raise a few eyebrows. Besides, Bastard guarded their goods. The horse would trample anyone who came meddling.

"Now," he said as he climbed up into the seat, "we see about getting you to one of the Houses of the Gods. Which one's yours?"

Maribel clambered up beside him. "Or I could stay with you."

He gave a single bark of laughter. "Slim chance, kid."

"Why? 'Cause I'm a girl?"

He snorted. "Hardly. I've known some bad ass women in my time."

"'Cause you think I can't take care of myself?"

"That'd be part of it, yeah."

"Well, I can!"

He gripped the reins in his hands but twisted to face her. "No, you can't. If you could, I wouldn't have needed to rescue you."

She stuck out her bottom lip in a pout, but shifted out of the sullen expression, turning bright and animated. "Teach me how to shoot a musket, and I can cook for you."

He smirked. "Do you even know what a stove is?"

This caused her face to contort with anger. "My ma taught me to be a proper wife, to sew and cook and take care of a house!"

Maro stared at her for a few moments, then nodded. "I believe you, but the trail's no place for—"

"A girl?" she interrupted.

"I was going to say lady." He glanced around them, watching what few people prowled the streets. There weren't but five buildings to this settlement, not counting what passed for the Houses of the Gods: a Bounty Hunter's Guild, a general goods store, a smithy, a saloon, and a stable—the extent of such a *prosperous* town.

The Houses of the Gods weren't much to look at, not out here. In the bigger cities, they were mausoleums of grandeur. In Red Creek, they were little more than shacks.

He flicked the reins, and the horses pulled out onto the road.

"So, which House is yours?" he asked again.

"Lust and Candor," she said with a glum voice.

"Really? Mine, too."

"See? We have things in common!"

"Belonging to the same religious House doesn't mean we have commonality, Maribel. It means we're two random schmoes who ended up in the same place."

"Everything happens for a reason."

He grunted.

"What? It's true!"

He grimaced. He hated to do it, but he needed to wash out that stupidity before she got herself in trouble later on in life. Maro leaned closer, almost coming down to her level.

"What was the reason for your parents' death?"

She glared up at him but didn't say a word. Her anger was almost palpable, and she kept her silence all the way to The House of Lust and Candor.

They pulled up a few minutes later, and by the time they rolled to a stop and Maro applied the brake, a man ambled out to greet them. He wore fine clothing that stood out from the locals. Maro had no idea what material they were made of, but it looked like silk, and the cobalt blues and crimson reds seemed garish compared to the muted earth tones of the population.

"Morning," the man said, his smile dazzling, flashing between the pair.

Maro grunted in response. Maribel stumbled out onto the wooden slats that served as a walkway. She took a position in front of the building and crossed her arms.

"The name's Roxald." The man glanced between them. "What brings you to the House this morning?"

"The girl."

"Don't call me girl!"

"Fine, Maribel."

A touch of a frown formed on Roxald's brow. "How can we help you?"

Maro climbed down, walked around the backside, and drew close. "Poor girl's orphaned. I brought her out here to live with her aunt and uncle. They perished, too. I've got no place to take her."

"You just don't want me because I'd be a nuisance," Maribel said.

"Damn right."

"I can cook and clean, do your laundry and make your bed; you wouldn't have to take care of me."

"Maribel, I don't have a home."

That caught her off guard, killing any further protest.

"I've got no job, no woman, and no home. I can't even take care of myself."

"So, we both have no homes," she mumbled in a quiet voice.

"More or less." Maro turned his attention to Roxald. "There's more to the story, but the girl needs to be taken in and cared for."

"We can most certainly do so for one of our own."

"I thought you were a good man, Maro."

He shook his head. "No, Maribel, I've never been a good man; I'm just trying to do a good deed."

"Don't call me that! My name's Amice. I told the banker that Maribel was my name because he scared me."

"Fine," he said, his voice soft, "so your name's different, but when I remember you, and I will, you'll always be Maribel to me."

"You won't let me stay with you?"

He shook his head.

"I hate you!"

She bolted for the front door of the House, slamming it behind her. Maro winced at the sound. In the cities, the doors were far too large and heavy for a child to shut, but out here, where the Houses were constructed from crude wood and barely the size of a general goods store, such a feat came easy.

The ex-soldier sighed. "Sorry about her."

Roxald smiled. "Quite alright. Kids are very impressionable, and they're the most honest out of everyone who walks Atar, often expressing what's in their hearts. She may be angry with you, but I doubt she'll hate you for long. One day, she'll look back and regret what she said in anger, and she'll know you are, indeed, a good man."

Maro stared at him for a moment. "Yeah, sure."

Roxald arched an eyebrow. "Want to tell me the full story?"

"Not really." He glanced back to the road, looking East towards Tepress. "But I will."

The ex-soldier gave him the tale, but he left out the gorier bits. Maro's soul was already stained, and there was no sense in ruining someone else's with the details. When he finished, the holy man looked a few shades paler.

Maro jumped into the back of the wagon, pulling Maribel's chest out from under the seat.

"I take it you don't want the guns?" he asked Roxald.

The clergyman shook his head.

"Thought not."

Maro opened the trunk and extracted them, placing them into his chest. Once locked again, he hopped out and pulled out Maribel's chest and placed it on the wooden planks with a thud. Lugging the heavy thing took his wind for a moment, but he couldn't show weakness, not in front of the clergyman. Then, he grabbed the puppy Maribel had taken from the ranch house and plopped the little fur ball beside the trunk.

"Well," Maro said, eyeing the road around him for traffic, "looks like this is the end of the line."

"It would appear so," Roxald said. "For the sake of your soul, when you get back to civilization, please go and repent at one of the Houses. Or come inside now, and I will aid your journey."

He gave a single harrumph. "The way I reckon, if the Everlasting Autarch's omniscient as implied, he already knows the status of my soul. It doesn't matter if I go to one of the Houses to talk to him, or if I do it around a campfire."

Maro checked to make sure Bastard's tether hadn't loosened, then climbed into his seat at the front, taking the reins in hand.

"Going to the House is the act of repentance, of humility for our transgressions, seeking peace only the Everlasting Autarch can grant. That's what matters."

He shrugged. "Perhaps." He blew out a breath from his nose. "What you don't understand, Father, is I ain't sorry. Someone had to do it, and I saved someone else's soul by doing the deed myself. And for humility," he pointed at his face, "I've got to walk around with this mug forever. I don't have a job, a home, a woman to love, or a kid to call my own. Probably never will. I'd say that's humbling enough. Take care of the girl. That'll give me peace."

Roxald swallowed and nodded. "You don't want to say goodbye to her?"

Maro shook his head. "She's got enough trauma for one life. No need to add to it."

With that, he flicked the reins, and the horses started out. Maro didn't glance back at the holy man, the House, or the little girl who ran away. That chapter was over, moments buried in the past, there to remember but never to relive. Now, he could only look ahead to the future.

He settled in as the wagon rumbled and rocked. It was going to be a long ride back to Tepress.

Epilogue

For those who seek gratification from children, who mutilate the adolescent for their own machinations, and those who coerce the young with falsehoods, there is no death horrible enough for you. Let none rest until every conceivable atrocity can be visited upon you—the Book of Morality, The Sacral Compendium.

One week later...

Maro pulled the brake on the wagon and climbed down to the road. He swayed for a moment, letting his body readjust to an unmoving ground. He stretched, reaching for the sky, coming up to his tiptoes before ambling to the back and Bastard. A cluster of soldiers stood laughing, and he had the sense of déjà vu. Hadn't he left these shitheads not two weeks before?

Is this how the main force of the army conducts themselves while I was out scouting and shitting in the woods?

Maro seethed at the injustice, but he stamped out the rising anger. That part of his life was over, just like escorting Maribel to Red Creek. His future, however clouded and uncertain, lay before him. Still, the urge to kick the shit out of the drunken fools did stir the embers within him.

I was never a good man, but I ain't a dumb one either.

The stockades would be the least of his worries if he gave into his baser instincts.

Untying Bastard, he led him to the hitching post, then dragged his saddle out and saddled him. With the trunk in his hands, he staggered up the three front steps to the guild and entered the building. It wasn't easy.

Nothing ever is.

Horace looked up from behind the counter as Maro came inside, and he did a double take.

"Well," Horace called, "I for sure thought the Lanton gang got ya."

Maro grunted as he closed the distance and hefted the trunk onto the countertop. "I went for the girl," he corrected, "but I took care of the gang."

Horace's eyes widened. "Bullshit."

Maro took off his wide-brim hat and set it on the counter. "I don't jest about killing since it seems the only thing I'm decent at."

Horace glanced at the trunk. "What's that?"

"Musket-pistols. There's five, but I plan to keep one. You can have the rest." He pointed out the window. "As well as the eight horses and the wagon."

Horace nodded. "That'll fetch a number of crowns. We can add that to the ledgers for you, but I count nine horses."

Maro shook his head. "Bastard's not for sale."

"You named your horse Bastard?"

He grunted, reached into his pocket, and produced the small, circular disc he claimed from Peredur, the bounty hunter who died on the trail. It spun on the countertop and clattered to a stop. "He's dead. Figured this might be the next best thing besides dragging his corpse back."

Horace plucked it from the wood and examined it. "How'd he die?"

"His guts were hanging out, but don't worry, I paid them back in full for taking the little girl."

"You saved her?"

He nodded once. "But the mastermind's still at large, and that's mainly because I didn't leave anyone alive to rat him out."

"Who's the mastermind?"

"Avardi."

"The banker?" The incredulous look on his face made it impossible for a blind man to miss. Horace cleared his throat, and from behind the counter, pulled out another disc similar to Peredur's. He handed it to Maro. The ex-soldier turned it over in his hands.

"So, if I take this, I'm a bounty hunter? I can pull wanted posters, buy and trade here?"

Horace nodded. "Minus your fee, of course, but with us taking in the pistols and the horses, I don't think you have to worry about that."

Maro stared at the chit for a long moment. He wanted to get away from this kind of life, the immoral killing, the torture, roughing it in the woods, but he wasn't a fool. Other than bounty hunting, he had no other prospects, no other way to make ends meet. But the posters, they were for men who were already found guilty in the sight of the law. Would tracking them down be immoral, or would he be carrying out their justice?

"Put it in your pocket," Horace said, his voice holding a stern edge. "You can worry over any dilemmas you have later. We're an extension of the lawmen, going after what they can't because they're too few. We enforce the law, not break it. That's what's different between us and them. Besides, there's always bounties for monsters, too. Most stay away from those due to the high mortality rate."

Maro cocked his head. "Monsters?"

Horace nodded. "Oh yeah, wargs, wraiths, trolls. You name it, we kill it."

Maro grunted and slipped the chit into his pocket.

"Now," Horace said, "why don't you tell me what happened out on the trail? And then, Drallus and I can help you find a way to nail Avardi."

"Who's Drallus?"

"The guild master here."

"Thought you were."

Horace shook his head.

Maro paused for a moment, considering where to start. What could he say? Would he spare Horace the gory details? If he did, his tale might not ring with truth. Instead, he decided to be as forthright as he could be, much more so than with the clergyman, and he'd spill every visceral fact.

"I had no qualms killing the gang," Maro started. "That was the easy part. A righteous man would've balked at the task, and an evil man would've joined them. That's why the Autarch made people like me, I guess, people who can purge Atar's filth. It doesn't surprise me that people like Avardi exist, and killing him outright will make me appear I'm as terrible as him."

"That's why you're going to tell me," Horace said, "and we'll figure out how to take him down together inside the law. But it won't be immediate, and it won't be easy."

I may not be a good man, but I can be better.

Maro grunted. "Nothing worth doing ever is."

About The Author

Kyle Belote is a prior active-duty Marine, writer, musician, and painter. He's lived in Texas, Hawaii, and Okinawa, Japan, and has traveled the globe before returning to the great Lone Star State. When not writing, he enjoys sketching, researching companies and investing, and reading/listening to audiobooks. Kyle enjoys a diverse collection of films, books, and shows.

For more information, please visit:
https://www.outpostdire.com/blogs
http://patreon.com/OutpostDire
Instagram: Outpost_Dire
Twitter: @outpostdire